"It doesn't matter that I'm your usual type, because I'm still the wrong woman."

"You got it." He flashed a half smile that melted that ball of ice in her stomach. "But then, I'm the wrong man for you." No half smile now. "And I'm pretty sure that makes this one of those irresistible situations we're just going to have to resist. Or at least keep reminding ourselves to do it."

Yes. She wondered, though, if a reminder would be just wasting mental energy. "I don't want to find you attractive." But she did. Mercy, did she. On a scale of one to ten, he was a six hundred, and even with the danger, he fired every nerve in her body.

JUSTICE IS COMING

USA TODAY Bestselling Author
DELORES FOSSEN

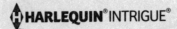
HARLEQUIN® INTRIGUE®

Recycling programs
for this product may
not exist in your area.

ISBN-13: 978-0-373-69728-1

JUSTICE IS COMING

Copyright © 2013 by Delores Fossen

Printed in U.S.A.

ABOUT THE AUTHOR

Imagine a family tree that includes Texas cowboys, Choctaw and Cherokee Indians, a Louisiana pirate and a Scottish rebel who battled side by side with William Wallace. With ancestors like that, it's easy to understand why *USA TODAY* bestselling author and former air force captain Delores Fossen feels as if she were genetically predisposed to writing romances. Along the way to fulfilling her DNA destiny, Delores married an air force top gun who just happens to be of Viking descent. With all those romantic bases covered, she doesn't have to look too far for inspiration.

Books by Delores Fossen

CAST OF CHARACTERS

Marshal Declan O'Malley—The youngest of six foster brothers raised in the notorious Rocky Creek orphanage, he comes face-to-face with a tragic past and his enemy, Eden Gray. She's the last woman on earth he wants to trust, but to keep them both alive, he must protect her. And his heart.

Eden Gray—A P.I. caught between protecting her father and an unexpected attraction for Declan, the cowboy lawman who could destroy her and her family.

Zander Gray—Eden's father. He's an escaped felon perhaps holding a grudge against Declan for arresting him.

Kirby Granger—Sixteen years ago this now-retired marshal rescued Declan and five other boys from the Rocky Creek orphanage, but he might have cut corners to do that.

Stella Doyle—Kirby's longtime friend. She, too, worked at Rocky Creek and might know more about the present danger than she's willing to admit.

Leonard Kane—A wealthy businessman who could be looking to settle some old scores with Kirby and Eden's father.

Jack Vinson—Stella's former fiancé. He might have helped Kirby get the boys out of Rocky Creek, but at what price?

Beatrice Vinson—Jack's wife, who's jealous of his old relationship with Stella. Her jealousy might have made her mentally unstable.

Chapter One

Marshal Declan O'Malley eased the saddle off his chestnut stallion. He tried not to make any sudden moves, and he didn't look over his shoulder, though Declan was pretty sure someone was watching him.

That "pretty sure" became a certainty when he spotted the footprints on the partially frozen ground.

What the heck was going on?

Since he'd been a federal marshal for nearly six years, he was accustomed to having people want to do him bodily harm, but threats like that rarely came right to his doorstep.

Or rather to his barn.

Declan put the saddle on the side of the watering trough and adjusted his buckskin jacket so he could reach the Colt in his belt holster. He gave the chestnut's rump a gentle slap, and as Declan had hoped he'd do, the stallion headed for some hay in the side corral. If there was going to be a shootout, Declan sure didn't want his horse caught up in the gunfire.

He stepped to the side of the barn door. And waited.

Listening.

But the only thing he could hear was the bitter December wind rattling the bare trees scattered around the grounds. He didn't mind the cold when he was on his daily ride, but he minded it a lot when he was waiting for something bad to happen.

Or maybe not bad.

He looked at the footprints again. Small. Like a woman's. He hadn't been in a relationship in the past three or four months, but maybe this was an old girlfriend come to visit. Still, it didn't feel like something that simple.

Or that fun.

His house wasn't exactly on the beaten path, not even by rural-Texas standards. He was literally on the back forty acres of his foster family's horse-and-cattle ranch. A good ten miles from the town of Maverick Springs, and with not even a paved road leading to his place. Besides, there wasn't much of value in his small wood-frame house to make it a target for thieves.

Declan glanced around. Kept listening. And when he was finally fed up with the cold, he drew his Colt and moved away from the barn door so he could follow those footprints. From the looks of it, the prints started at the back of his barn, and that meant somebody had probably walked in from the pasture and checked out the barn itself.

Maybe looking for him.

Or looking to make sure he'd indeed gone on his daily ride.

And then the trespasser had made her way to the back of his house. Declan went in that direction now, using the trees for cover.

Finally, he saw something.

Or rather *someone*.

There was a person dressed in dark clothes and equally dark sunglasses peering around the edge of his back porch. Judging from her size, it was probably a woman, though he couldn't be positive since his visitor was wearing a black baseball cap slung low on her head, and the brim covered most of her face. Declan expected her to duck out of sight when she spotted him.

She didn't.

She put her index finger to her mouth in a keep-quiet gesture.

What the hell?

And just to confuse things even more, she motioned for him to come closer.

Declan debated it. He debated calling out to her, too, but she frantically shook her head and made that keep-quiet gesture again.

He looked to see if she was armed. Couldn't tell. But since she'd had ample opportunity to shoot at him and hadn't, Declan decided to take his chances. He didn't put his gun away, but he went closer.

Yeah, it was a woman all right. About five-six, with an average build. Judging from the strands of hair that had slipped out from the back of the baseball cap, she was a brunette.

"Inside," she whispered and tipped her head to his back door. *"Please,"* she added.

Well, if she was a criminal, she was a polite one, that was for sure. The *please* didn't sway Declan one bit, but her shaky voice did. There was fear in it. Or something. Something that told him she wasn't a killer.

Well, probably not.

He'd been wrong before. And he had the scar on his chest to prove it.

But did that stop him?

Much to his disgust, nope, it didn't. He'd never been a cautious man, and while this seemed like a really good time to start, Declan went even closer, still looking for any sign that she was armed.

Okay, she was.

Without any prompting, his mysterious visitor opened the side of her jacket to show him the gun—a Glock—that she had tucked in a shoulder holster. Since she made no attempt to draw it, Declan walked even closer, up the side steps. He also tapped the badge he had pinned to his holster, just in case she didn't know she was dealing with a deputy U.S. marshal.

She kept her head down so he still didn't have a good look at her face. "I know exactly who you are, Declan O'Malley," she whispered.

Well, that wasn't much of a stretch. Everyone in Maverick Springs knew who he was. He and his five foster brothers, who were all marshals, too. Anyone could have found out his name and where he lived within minutes after arriving in town. Heck, he didn't even have a burglar alarm because he figured no one would be stupid enough to do what this woman was apparently trying to do.

"Inside," she repeated.

It wasn't caution but rather common sense that had him staying put when she turned toward his door. "I want answers first," he insisted.

"Shh." The fear in her body language went up a significant notch, and she fired a few nervous glances around his yard.

Confused and now somewhat riled at, well, whatever the heck this was, Declan followed her glances but didn't see anything out of the ordinary. Only the woman.

He cupped her chin, lifted it.

And groaned.

Yeah. He recognized her all right, and it wasn't a good kind of recognition, either.

Eden Gray.

What in the Sam Hill was she doing here at his house?

He opened his mouth to demand some answers but her hand flew up, and she pressed her fingers to his mouth. Cold fingers at that.

But soft.

And she smelled like some kind of girlie hand lotion. It definitely didn't go with that Glock she was carrying or the fact that she was trespassing.

"They might hear you," she whispered. "Inside," she insisted again.

"They?"

She eased down her fingers, stepped back and yanked off her glasses. Those eyes caught him off guard for just a moment. Ice blue but somehow without a hint of cold in them. Definitely memorable, but he hadn't needed to see her eyes to know this was a blast from his past that he didn't want or need.

Well, a blast he didn't need anyway.

For a split second, his body overrode his brain, and that whole *want* thing came into play. In those brief moments, he didn't see Eden Gray, a person who despised him, but rather a hot woman. One who just happened to be armed and acting crazy.

She swallowed hard.

Something different went through her eyes. Not fear, but Declan recognized the look. It was the quick glance that a woman gave a man when she was interested but didn't want to be.

Declan was afraid he was giving her the same look right back. *Oh, man.* One day he was going to learn to think with his head only and not some other body part that often got him into trouble.

She swallowed hard again. Turned. And she eased open the door. *Sorry,* she mouthed.

Declan didn't ask for what. He didn't want to know. He only wanted answers, and that was why he followed her inside to his kitchen.

"Why are you here?" he demanded.

But she still didn't answer. She hurried to the window over his sink and looked out. She did another of those shifty glances that he often did when he was doing surveillance or in the presence of danger.

"You obviously remember me," she finally said.

He gave her a flat look. *"Obviously."*

"This way," Eden added. "I have to show you something." And she headed toward his living room that was only a few yards away.

She would have made it there, too, but Declan snagged her by the arm and whirled her back around to face him. "Remembering you doesn't tell me why you're here. Now spill it, or I'm tossing you out."

"You can't." Eden was breathing through her mouth now, and her pulse was jumping in her throat. But that didn't stop her from shaking off his grip, catching his arm and pulling him into the living room.

"Stay away from the windows," she warned.

Just on principle and because he was now about twelve steps past being ornery, Declan considered doing the opposite of anything she was asking. "Give me a reason why I should stay away from my own window."

"There's a tiny camera attached to the big oak on the right side of your front porch." Her breath trembled in her throat. "And they're watching the front of the house. Maybe trying to listen, too."

Declan shook his head, stared at her and made a circling motion with his gun for her to continue. He needed more. A lot more, but he needed that "a lot more" to make sense. So far, that wasn't happening.

"Did you miss a dose of meds or something?" he asked.

"No." She stretched that out a few syllables. "I'm not crazy. And I have a good reason for being here."

He stared at her, made the circling motion with his hand again.

"I got here about a half hour ago, while you were out riding," she said. "I've watched you for the past two days, so I know you take a ride this time of morning before you go in to work."

Well, it was an answer all right, but it didn't answer much. "You watched me?"

She nodded.

"Really?" And he didn't take the skepticism out of it, either.

Until this morning when he'd reined in at the barn, he hadn't felt or seen anyone watching him yesterday or the day before. Of course, he'd had a lot on his mind what with his foster father, Kirby Granger, battling cancer. The thought of losing Kirby had been weighing on him. Maybe enough for him to not notice someone stalking him.

He looked her straight in the eye. "Are you going to make me arrest you, or do you plan to keep going with that explanation?"

She made a soft sound of frustration, looked out the window again. "I'm a P.I. now. I own a small agency in San Antonio."

She'd skipped right over the most important detail of her brief bio. "Your father's Zander Gray, a lowlife swindling scum. I arrested him about three years ago for attempting to murder a witness who was going to testify against him, and he was doing hard time before he escaped."

And this was suddenly becoming a whole lot clearer.

"He sent you here," Declan accused.

"No," she quickly answered. "I'm not even sure he's alive."

Okay, maybe not so clear after all.

"But my father might have been the reason they contacted me in the first place," Eden explained. "They might have thought I'd do anything to get back at you for arresting him. I won't."

He made a sound of disagreement. "Since you're trespassing and have been stalking me, convince me otherwise that you're not here to avenge your father."

"I'm not." Not a whisper that time. And there was some fire in those two little words. "But someone's trying to set me up. Earlier this week someone broke into my office, planted some fake financials on my computer and changed the password so I can't delete them from the server. That someone is trying to make it look as if I'm funneling money to a radical militia group buying illegal firearms."

Declan thought about that a second. "Lady, if you wanted me to investigate that, you didn't have to follow me or come to my ranch. My office is on Main Street in town."

Another headshake. "They didn't hire me to go to your office."

Mercy. It was hard to hang on to his temper with this roundabout conversation. "There it is again. That *they.* *They* put up the camera that you don't want me to go to the window and see. So who are they?"

"I honestly don't know." She dodged his gaze, tried to turn away, but he took hold of her again and forced her to face him. "After I realized someone had planted that false info on my computer, I got a call from a man using a prepaid cell phone. I didn't recognize his voice. He said if I went to the cops or the marshals, he'd release the info on my computer and I'd be arrested."

And maybe she would be. Because some cops might assume like father, like daughter.

But was she?

Declan pushed that question aside. Right now, that didn't matter. "This unknown male caller is the one who put the camera outside?"

"I think so. If not him, then someone working with or for him. All I know is it's there because I saw a man wearing a ski mask installing it right after you left for your ride."

He shook his head. "If they sent you to watch me, why use a camera?"

"Because the camera is to watch *me*," she clarified. "To make sure I do what he ordered me to do."

"And what exactly are you supposed to do?" Declan demanded.

Eden Gray shoved her hand over her Glock. "Kill you."

Chapter Two

Declan O'Malley came at her so fast that Eden didn't even see it coming until it was too late.

Even though he was tall and lanky, he still packed a wallop when he slammed into her, knocking her back against the wall. In the same motion, he ripped her gun from her shoulder holster, tossed it behind him and jammed his own weapon beneath her chin.

"Kill me?" His teeth were clenched now. Jaw, too. And even though there were no lights on in the living room, she had no trouble seeing the venom in his eyes.

Eden was certain there was no venom in hers. Just fear. It'd been a huge risk coming here. From everything she'd read and heard about him, Declan could be a dangerous man. Still, she hadn't had a choice. If she was going to die, she'd rather it be at his hands than others'.

"The man who called me on the burner cell ordered me to kill you," Eden managed to say. Though it was hard to speak with the marshal's body pressed against her chest. It was hard to breathe, too.

But maybe Declan himself was responsible for that.

Eden had known that he fell into the drop-dead-hot category. Tall, dark, deadly. However, what she hadn't known was that despite the danger and this insane situation, she would feel the punch of attraction. She'd never expected to feel it for this man, but it was there.

You're losing it, Eden.

Declan O'Malley was the job. For some huge reasons, especially one, he couldn't be anything else.

"Why does he want me dead?" he demanded.

"I don't know. That's the truth," Eden added when he made a "yeah, right" sound. "He just told me if I didn't kill you that he'd release the info he planted on my computer."

No "yeah, right" this time, but his left eyebrow lifted. "You'd kill me rather than risk charges for funneling money to a militia group?"

Eden lifted her own eyebrow. She wasn't feeling especially brave, definitely not like the cocky man looming in front of her. The seconds were ticking away, and with each one of them, the risk got higher and higher. Someway, somehow, she had to get this hot cowboy marshal to go along with an asinine plan that had little or no chance of succeeding.

Still, little was better than zero.

Without warning, he yanked the baseball cap from her head and threw it in the direction her Glock had landed. Her hair was in a ponytail, but it dropped against her shoulder. He studied it. Then her eyes. Every inch of her face. Maybe trying to figure out if she was telling him the truth. Or maybe he was just giving her the twice over as she'd done to him.

She hoped not.

They didn't need both of them feeling this involuntary heat.

"You sure this isn't about your father?" he pressed.

"I'm sure. I haven't heard from him since he escaped from jail."

And she didn't want to get into that sore subject now. Declan had arrested her father, and then her father had escaped. It wouldn't do any good to mention that she believed her father was innocent of at least the most serious charge—attempted murder. That really wouldn't help in getting Declan to cooperate if she questioned his lawman's skills of apprehending a guilty suspect.

"Could you at least move the gun?" Eden asked. "Because we need to talk. I figure at most I've got twenty minutes left before someone will want to know why I haven't fired a shot."

She was being generous with that timeline. The mysterious caller had told her to show Declan ASAP what she'd been sent. Why, she didn't know, but it seemed as if that was only to taunt him.

Or rile him even more than he already was.

Like poking an ornery rattler with a short stick. It hardly seemed wise, but she would show him. And hope for a way out of this.

Declan slid his intense green eyes to the gun, then back to her. "Yes to the talking. No to moving the gun."

There was just a touch of an Irish brogue beneath that Texas drawl. A strange combination. And one she might have enjoyed hearing if his finger wasn't on the trigger of the gun pressed to her throat.

"I agreed to kill you because I didn't have a choice," Eden explained. No beautiful lilt to her words. Her voice was strained like the rest of her. One big giant nerve. "If the planted info had been leaked, it would have set off an opposing militia group that would in turn kill me, the rest of my family and anyone they thought might be a friend of mine."

Finally, he let up a little on the pressure to her chest and eased back a fraction. Still close. Still touching. He probably hadn't realized that he had his right leg shoved between hers. Eden's gaze drifted in that direction. Then back up at Declan.

Correction. He'd noticed.

But clearly he didn't plan to do anything about the intimate contact between them.

"I have two sisters," she added. "They're nineteen and twenty. Barely adults, and they've been through more than enough with my father's arrest and disappearance. They don't deserve to die because someone's targeting you."

"You could have arranged for them and you to be protected," he pointed out.

"I did the best I could, but there's no place to hide from these men. Eventually they'd get through any security I could set up. They proved that by hacking into my computer and leaving that bogus info."

Declan made another sound that led her to believe he was making fun of her.

"You ever killed a man before?" he challenged, but he didn't wait for Eden to answer. "My guess is no."

He put his face right next to hers. So close that the brim of his midnight-black Stetson scraped against her forehead. It was hard to tell where the Stetson ended and his hair began, because they were the same color.

"And my second guess is that you can't kill me," he went on. "Of course, that's not really a guess since I wouldn't let you get the chance."

"I wasn't planning to kill you," she said, but had to clear her throat and repeat it so it'd have sound. Great. She was acting like a wuss rather than a P.I. with her family's lives, and hers, at stake.

"You're here with a gun," he reminded her.

"I didn't intend to use it. Well, not to shoot you anyway. I will have to fire, though, because I want whoever's on the other end of that camera to believe you're dead. And to make sure that person doesn't come in here and try to do the job himself, I need to fire soon."

With his gaze still pinned to hers, he backed up again. "Maybe we should do just that—let the person come in here and try to kill me," he suggested. "If he's really out there. He won't get far. I'm thinking a step in the house. Two at most. And I wouldn't let him get off the first shot."

"I don't doubt it. But I can't risk that. His death could start a chain reaction that'll get my sisters killed."

Thankfully, he didn't disagree with that. Well, not verbally anyway. "Tell me everything you know about the person who hired you to do this."

"There isn't time." Eden tried to look out the window to make sure no one was coming, but the angle was wrong. "He said I had to have the job done by seven-thirty. It's seven-twenty now."

"Make time," he countered.

Eden huffed and tried to think of the fastest explanation. It wasn't too hard because she didn't know a lot of facts. "I don't have a clue who he is. As I said, he used an untraceable cell phone. It's the same with the info he emailed me about you. I tried to track down the source, but it led me to a coffee shop in San Antonio where hundreds of people use the internet each day. There aren't any security cameras and no surveillance feed from nearby businesses."

He gave her another hard look. "What info about me did he email you?"

"It's on my phone."

Eden glanced in the direction of her pocket, where his hip was still brushing against hers. She waited until he nodded before she reached between them, and the back of her hand did more than brush. She had no choice but to touch him in a place that she shouldn't be touching.

He still didn't back away.

But Declan did make a slight sound of discomfort.

Eden knew how he felt. This wasn't comfortable for her, either, and it was even worse because touching him wasn't nearly as unpleasant as it should have been. After all, he was holding her at gunpoint.

Still, it was time to poke that rattler.

She went through the emails on her phone until she reached the first one the man had sent her. It was a series of photos with just four words: Your target, Declan O'Malley.

She went through the shots, the first a recent one of him wearing his gun and badge and going into the marshals' building in Maverick Springs. It appeared to have been taken from a camera with a long-range lens.

Eden showed Declan the photo and went to the next one, a close-up of him at the diner across the street from his office. Probably taken with the same long-range camera since it had a grainy texture.

"Did you have any idea you were being photographed?" she asked, hoping that maybe he'd seen the person who'd snapped these shots.

Declan shook his head, and while his expression didn't change much, Eden figured that had to bother him. It was a violation, something she knew loads about since this whole computer-hacking incident.

She clicked to another photo of Declan in his truck, turning onto the road that led to his foster family's ranch and to his own place. The next shot was of his license plate.

And then Eden got to the last one.

The puzzling one.

It was an old wedding photo of four adults and a young boy. Even though the person who'd emailed it to her hadn't identified by name all the people in the group shot, he had said that the child was Declan. He was about four years old, dressed in his Sunday best, and the people surrounding him were his parents, an uncle and the uncle's bride. They were all smiling. A happy-family photo.

It didn't make Declan happy now.

He closed his eyes for just a split second, and then he cursed, using some really foul language. And Eden knew why. She, too, was personally familiar with bad memories. And despite the smiles, this photo was indeed a bad memory, because in less than twenty-four hours after it'd been taken, Declan's life had turned on a dime.

Or rather turned on a different kind of metal.

Some bullets.

"The information this hacker gave me was that the photo was of your family in Germany," Eden said. "They were all murdered when you were four years old."

Declan took a moment, inhaled a slightly deeper breath. "Why the hell did he send you that?"

Eden shook her head. "I was hoping you could tell me. The person also said your name had been changed after the murders."

"It was. Twice. But as far as I know, no other living person has that specific information. Except maybe my family's killer."

Was that it? Was that the connection?

"What does this photo have to do with the order the hacker gave me to kill you?" she asked.

He snatched the phone from her, backed up, but he still didn't lower his gun. He kept it aimed right at her while he glanced out the window. Maybe to see if the camera installer was returning. He apparently wasn't, because Declan's attention went back to the photos. There weren't more to see, but he paused for a long time on that last one.

The bad-memory one.

"I've been digging, but I don't have many answers," she admitted. "Still, I have to believe that picture has something to do with all of this or he wouldn't have sent it to me."

Eden paused, hoping Declan didn't shoot her for asking what she had to ask. "What do you remember about your family's murders? Who killed them? Because the person sent me links of the old crime, but all the articles said the culprit was an unknown assailant."

A sterile term for something far from sterile.

"I don't know who killed them." He was in control again. The tough cowboy lawman, and he was glaring at her, maybe because he didn't believe she was innocent in all of this.

And maybe she wasn't.

Eden didn't know if she was one hundred percent blameless, but that was what she intended to find out—after she bought herself and her sisters some time.

"I don't have any memories of the attack," Declan finally added. "According to the shrink the cops made me see, I blocked them out."

Too bad. But Eden cringed at the thought. Maybe blocking them out had been the only way Declan had survived. That and being hidden in a cellar while his family was murdered. If he hadn't been in that cellar, he would have been killed, as well. In fact, Eden was afraid that Declan was the reason they'd been killed in the first place.

Judging from the look in his eyes, he thought so, too.

He groaned, dropped back another step and shoved her phone in his front pocket. Maybe so he'd have a free hand to scrub over his face—which he did.

"What's the first memory you do have after the murders?" she asked.

"A few days later." And that was all he said for several long moments. "The local cops put me in protective custody, gave me a fake name and eventually sent me to a distant cousin, Meg Tanner, in Ireland. I lived on and off with her and then some of her friends in County Clare for eight years before she brought me to Texas."

Yes, because Meg had learned she had Parkinson's disease and could no longer take care of Declan. Or at least that was the info Eden had been given by the mystery person who'd orchestrated this visit to Declan's place.

"Eventually your cousin took you to the Rocky Creek Children's Facility," Eden supplied. "Why there?"

"She just said I'd be safe there. I got another name, the one I use now, and Kirby said I shouldn't talk about my past to anyone. So I didn't."

Eden took up the rest of the explanation. "The facility didn't normally take boys your age, but they made an exception. Actually, someone there faked the paperwork so you could be admitted."

Declan glared again. "How do you know that?"

"Despite what you think of me, I'm a good P.I. I know how to find information, even when someone wants that information hidden."

Though it had been especially challenging to get any records from the notorious facility because of an ongoing investigation into the murder of the orphanage's headmaster, Jonah Webb. According to what she'd learned,

Webb's wife had murdered him sixteen and a half years ago when Declan was just thirteen years old and his five foster brothers had all been living at Rocky Creek.

And Webb's wife had an unknown accomplice.

Declan and all five of his foster brothers were suspects. So was their foster father, Kirby Granger, the retired marshal who had "rescued" Declan and his foster brothers and then raised them on his sprawling ranch.

That led Eden to her next question. "Is this connected to Jonah Webb's murder investigation?"

Declan certainly didn't jump to deny it, and coupled with that photo of him as a child, this might be one very complex puzzle. Something they didn't have time for right now.

"I need to fire the gun," Eden reminded him, checking the time again. "The person who set this up needs to believe you're dead."

"So you've said," he argued.

Eden was sure her mouth dropped open. "You don't believe me?"

"Why should I?"

It took her a moment to get control of her voice so she could speak. "Why else would I have come here? Why else would I have those pictures of you?"

Declan gave her a flat look. "You tell me."

Oh, mercy. She hadn't expected Declan to blindly go along with the faked-death plan, but Eden had figured the photos would have at least convinced him that he was in danger. And not from her. But from the same person who could get her and her sisters killed the hard way.

She walked closer to him. "Look, I don't want to be here, and I darn sure don't want to be involved in this mess. I have enough going on in my life—"

"Enough going on that you could have cut a deal with someone to kill me. I've made enemies."

Yes, he had made enemies. Plenty of them. For whatever reason, maybe old baggage from his childhood, Declan volunteered to take the worst cases. Scum of the scum. And men like that didn't forgive and forget easily. They would often try to take revenge against the lawman who'd arrested them.

"I'm not disputing that people might want you dead," Eden said. "But why come to me? Why involve me in this other than because you arrested my father? I think even you have to admit that's a thin connection."

"Maybe." Clearly, he wasn't admitting that at all. He reached down, picked up her gun and shoved it into the waistband of his jeans. "Come on. You're going to the marshals' office with me so I can take a statement."

Eden held her ground when he latched on to her arm. "Someone wants to kill you." Though she'd already made that point several times. Either he didn't believe her at all or he was ready to risk his life and hers by walking out that door.

"Think of my sisters," she said, and she was ready to beg if necessary. "You know what it's like to lose someone close to you. Don't make my family go through that."

Eden didn't see what she wanted in his eyes—any indication that he was considering what she'd just asked. But then Declan turned his gun toward the floor.

And fired.

The two shots blasted through the small house, the bullets tearing into the wood floor. The sound was deafening. Unnerving.

But a relief, too.

"Thank you," Eden managed to say despite her suddenly bone-dry throat. "Now, for the next step. While you pretend to be dead, I'll leave and contact one of your brothers. I'm thinking maybe Harlan McKinney." She'd researched them all, and he seemed the most levelheaded.

He shook his head. "I'll call Wyatt. Harlan's tied up with some personal stuff right now. Wedding plans," he added in a mumble. His gaze shot back to hers. "I've got no intention of playing dead for long. You cooperate with Wyatt and me, and we'll get to the bottom of this."

Before she could agree, Declan got in her face again. "Here's the only warning you'll get from me. If you're lying about any of this, I *will* make you pay."

She nodded, knowing that this was far from over. It was just the beginning, and Eden prayed they could all get out of it alive.

Using his left hand, Declan took out his phone from his pocket. Hopefully to call his foster brother Wyatt McCabe, but he didn't press any buttons or numbers. Declan froze for a moment before his gaze shifted to the window.

Eden's heart went to her knees. "Did you hear something?"

"Yeah." He hooked his arm around her and shoved her behind him.

That only made her racing heart worse, and she came up on her toes to try to look over his shoulder. She didn't have to look far.

Eden spotted someone beside the tree where that camera had been mounted. A man. He was peering through a scope on a rifle.

And he had that rifle aimed right at Declan O'Malley's house.

Chapter Three

Declan backed Eden deeper into the shadows and took aim out the window. The guy didn't appear to be on the verge of shooting, but Declan didn't want to take any chances. If this moron fired, it would be the last shot he'd ever take.

Without moving his attention from the man with that rifle, Declan pushed the button on his phone to call his foster brother Wyatt.

"You still at the ranch?" Declan asked the moment Wyatt answered.

"Yeah. About to leave for work now. Why?"

"I got a problem. Several of them, in fact." He spared Eden a glance to make sure she wasn't ready to do anything stupid. Her attention, too, was staked to the guy outside, and judging from her reaction, his being there wasn't part of her plan.

Whatever her plan was.

Just in case her plan was to still kill him, Declan repositioned her so that she was hip to hip with him. He didn't want her in his line of sight in case she tried to grab her Glock from his jeans.

"A man has a rifle pointed at my house," Declan explained to his brother. "I need you out here, but make a quiet approach from the back. I'd do it myself, but I have another unexpected visitor. This one's inside, and it's Zander Gray's daughter."

Wyatt cursed. "What the hell's going on?"

"Not sure yet, but I'm about to find out." Declan used the camera on his phone to click a picture of the guy, and he fired it off to Wyatt. "Send that to Dallas and see if we can get a hit on facial recognition. I need it fast. Oh, and if possible, keep the guy outside alive. I need to question him."

"I'll try," Wyatt assured him.

Declan had no doubt that Wyatt would indeed try, and it shouldn't take him long to get to Declan's place, since the main ranch house was less than a mile away. Wyatt would hurry, too. No doubts about that.

"You recognize that man with the rifle?" Declan asked Eden the moment he ended the call with Wyatt.

"No." She didn't hesitate, either. "But I warned you that someone was likely watching."

Yeah, someone who wanted to make sure she murdered him.

But there were some huge holes in her story. For instance, if someone had wanted him dead, why send a female P.I. with a goody-two-shoes voice and a body that could distract a man? A face, too.

Maybe that was exactly why someone had sent her.

Declan had never hurt a woman, even one that he'd butted heads with. And it could be the person behind all of this thought Eden might be able to pull the trigger before he even saw it coming.

Declan motioned for her to take out her phone when he felt it vibrate. She pulled it out, and her breath stalled when she saw the screen.

"The caller blocked the number," she relayed.

The guy with the rifle had both hands on his weapon,

so he wasn't making the call, but it could be coming from the person who'd hired this would-be triggerman and Eden, as well.

"Answer it," Declan insisted. "And put it on speaker."

She nodded, and her hand was trembling when she clicked the buttons. Eden didn't say anything. She just waited for the caller to respond, and she didn't have to wait long.

"You there, Gray?" the caller asked her. A man.

Declan used his phone to record the call so he could have it analyzed. Hopefully it wouldn't be needed as part of a murder investigation—Declan's own or Eden's.

"I'm here," she answered. "I'm sure you heard the shots. O'Malley's dead, so give me the password to delete the lies you planted on my computer."

That request meshed with the story she'd told Declan, but he wasn't ready to believe her just yet. For reasons he didn't yet understand, all of this—including her response to this call—could be part of her plan.

"Can't give you anything without proof," the caller argued. "I'm sending in someone to see the body."

"There's not enough time for that," Eden answered before Declan could coach her on what to say. "O'Malley managed to get off a call to the marshals. They're on the way. Best if we all get out of here now."

Declan gave her the worst glare he could manage, because that was not the way he wanted this to go down. He wanted the gunman to come inside the house. Or rather he wanted the gunman to try. Then Declan could have disarmed him and arrested his sorry butt so he could interrogate him. He darn sure didn't want the guy running off.

"The marshals?" the caller growled. "How much time before they arrive?"

Maybe the glare worked, because she hesitated. "I'm not sure."

Declan pointed toward the rifleman and then toward his front door. "Tell him to come in," he mouthed.

After a long hesitation, she gave another shaky nod. "You should have time to check the body if you make it quick."

But the caller didn't jump at the chance to do that. "I have a better idea. You go ahead and get out of there, and I'll verify O'Malley's dead once you're gone. Wouldn't want the marshals to catch you."

There was a taunting edge to his tone, but he didn't give Eden a chance to come back with a response. "Leave now," the caller said. "Walk out the front door and head straight for your car that you left on the ranch trail. If you go anywhere but there, our deal is off." He ended the call.

Eden pulled in a long breath. "I'd like my gun before I go outside."

Declan looked at her as if she'd lost her mind. "The caller doesn't believe you killed me," he pointed out. "And the moment you walk out that door, his hired gun will bring you down before you can blink. You're a loose end, and he's not going to let you live."

In fact, that had maybe been part of the plan all along. Somehow, convince Eden to kill him and then they'd kill her. That didn't answer his question of why, but Declan figured he could get to that soon enough.

If he kept them alive, that is.

"He'll try to kill me," Eden agreed. "But I'm not a bad shot. Plus, I know he's out there. I can fire as soon as I step on the porch."

"Even if you're the best shot in the state, that's a stupid plan. He's already got the rifle aimed and ready, and you don't even know if he's alone. If he misses, which I doubt he will, he could have a friend or two ready to make sure you die."

Her eyes practically doubled in size. "Oh, God," she mumbled.

Yeah. *Oh, God.*

Thankfully, Wyatt would be expecting the worst and knew how to sneak up to the house without being seen.

"So what do we do?" she asked. "We can't just wait. He'll be expecting me to walk out there."

"Then he'll be disappointed, won't he? If he wants you dead—and I'm pretty sure he does—then he can send his lackey in to do the job."

She mumbled another "Oh, God," and practically slumped against him. "This could have been all about me. Maybe to set me up for your murder. Maybe *I* made the wrong enemy."

"That's one real good possibility. Or it could be he wants us both dead. A two-birds-with-one-stone kind of deal. Maybe we both made the wrong enemies."

But why had this moron sent her the pictures of him? Especially that one photo of him and his family? The image of it was branded into his head, but seeing it again had brought the nightmare flooding back.

Hell.

After all these years, the nightmare was still there even though he had no memories of the day his family had been murdered. No clues to give the cops to help them find the person or persons responsible. Ironic, since his life now was all about finding justice for others, and he hadn't found it for his own kin.

"When the person called you to set all of this up, did he give you any other details about my family?" Declan asked.

"No." Eden made a soft sound of frustration. "But I did a background check to see if I could find any connection. I couldn't." She paused. "I couldn't even find a record of your birth parents."

Because there wasn't one, and Declan should know because he'd searched for it for years. His cousin, Meg, had disappeared after she'd abandoned him at the Rocky Creek facility. That meant Declan had no idea if he even had any living relatives.

"When I was a kid, I asked anyone who might know something about my mom and dad," he told her, "but I never got any answers."

"Maybe the person who killed your family is behind this."

Yeah. More of the nightmare. The killer returning, and this time there'd be no cellar. No place to hide. But he wasn't a little boy any longer. He was a federal marshal who'd been trained by the best: his foster dad, Kirby. Declan could take care of himself, but at the moment, that wasn't his biggest worry.

The killer could go after his family again.

His new family. The one he'd had since he'd left Rocky Creek sixteen years ago.

His brothers—Dallas, Clayton, Harlan, Slade and Wyatt—could also protect themselves, but Kirby was another matter. He was weak from chemo treatments and couldn't fight off a fly. His long-time friend, Stella, was in the same boat. No chemo for her, but Declan figured she wasn't capable of taking on hired guns, especially now. Both Kirby and she were no doubt still at the Maverick Springs hospital for an overnight stay, where Kirby was getting his latest round of treatments.

Just the thought of someone hurting Kirby had Declan reaching for his phone again, but it buzzed before he could make a call and have someone go to the hospital.

"You've got more than two problems, little brother," Wyatt immediately greeted him. "In addition to the rifle guy out front, there's another one on the west side of the house, right by the road that leads off the ranch."

Oh, man. One gunman and a P.I. that he maybe couldn't trust were bad enough, but now there was a third piece in this dangerous puzzle.

"Clayton's on the way," Wyatt added.

Declan didn't want that, even if he might need the extra backup. "Send him to the hospital to guard Kirby."

"You think he's in danger?"

"Could be." And it sickened Declan to even think that.

"My sisters need protection, too," Eden blurted out. "Trish and Alice Gray. They're both students at the University of Texas. I have a bodyguard watching them, but it might not be enough."

Her plea certainly sounded convincing, but Declan wasn't about to give her blanket trust just yet.

He heard Wyatt make a call and request the protection for all three—Kirby and the Gray sisters. Declan was hoping it was overkill, but he had a sickening feeling that this situation had already gotten out of hand.

"Try to neutralize the guy on the road," Declan instructed his brother. "I'll deal with the one out front." He didn't wait for his brother to agree. Wyatt would.

Declan shoved his phone into his pocket. "Wait here."

Eden was shaking her head before he even finished. "I can give you some backup."

"No. You'll stay here." Declan didn't leave much room for argument, though he briefly considered returning her gun just in case the guy managed to get in the front door. However, there was that part about him not trusting her.

He took her by the arm and practically shoved her behind his sofa. "Stay put, and that's not a suggestion."

Whether she would or not was anyone's guess, but Declan couldn't worry about that now. He had to take care of this situation and then check on Kirby.

Declan locked the front door, though it wouldn't stop a gunman from shooting through the wood and getting inside.

With Eden.

And that was what Declan couldn't let happen, especially if it turned out that she was just a pawn in all of this. Even if she wasn't a pawn, she could still have the answers he needed to figure out what the heck was going on.

He grabbed some extra ammo for his Colt from the top of his fridge, crammed it in his coat pocket and headed to the back door. He looked out to make sure there wasn't another gunman lying in wait.

The backyard appeared to be empty, so Declan eased open the door and stepped onto the porch. He took a moment, listening, but didn't hear any unusual sounds.

He hurried down the steps and to the side of the house. Using it for cover, he looked out and spotted the tree with the small camera mounted on the branch. The rifleman was there, beneath that camera, and he still had both his gun and attention fastened to the front of the house. Declan had a clear look at his face, but it wasn't familiar. Maybe they'd get lucky with the recognition software or the interrogation he planned to do once he had these dirtbags in custody.

Declan froze when he heard something. Footsteps.

But not from outside. They were coming from inside the house, and he cursed Eden for not listening to him. Maybe, just maybe, she wouldn't do something stupid like walk outside.

The thought had no sooner crossed his mind than he heard the back door open, and he saw Eden step out onto the porch. She had a gun. A little Smith & Wesson that she'd probably had concealed somewhere on her body. He cursed again. Damn. He should have taken the time to frisk her.

Too late for that now, though.

Declan caught the movement from the corner of his eye. From the guy with the rifle. The man stood. Not slow and easy, either. He flew to a standing position, and with that same lightning speed, he pivoted directly toward Declan.

And took aim.

"Get down!" Declan yelled to Eden.

He dived back behind the house, toward the porch and Eden, just as she dropped to the weathered wooden planks. She hadn't even gotten fully down when the sound blasted through the air.

A shot.

And it hadn't come from the direction of the rifleman but rather the west side of his property.

Where his brother had spotted the other gunman.

A jolt of fear went through Declan. Not for himself but for Wyatt. Maybe his brother had been ambushed, because that wasn't a shot fired from the Colt that Wyatt would almost certainly be carrying.

Declan turned and tried to pick through the woods to see if he could spot the shooter. But there came another blast. And another. Not from the west this time.

The shots slammed into the side of his house and porch.

Hell.

Eden and he were caught in the crossfire of a gunfight.

Chapter Four

Eden's heart slammed against her chest. The blasts from those shots roared through her entire body. And she wasn't sure what she should do to get herself out of the line of fire.

Declan made the decision for her.

He took hold of her arm and dragged her off the porch and onto the steps, just inches from where he was trying to watch both the back and side of the house. Eden kept a firm grip on her backup weapon, and even though she landed in a sprawl, she levered herself up enough so that she could take aim.

"Don't shoot," Declan snarled, snagging her hand again. "My brother's out there."

Yes, but out there where? Eden's gaze fired all around them, but she couldn't see his brother or the shooters, only the bullets as they pelted into the frozen ground and porch.

"How soon before your brother can move closer and help us get out of this?" she asked.

"Maybe not soon enough." Declan turned slightly and fired a shot in the direction of the gunman in the tree. "Why the hell did you come out here anyway?"

Her heart was pounding in her ears, and it took her

a few seconds to actually hear that question. "Because I don't trust you."

The glance he gave her could have frozen fire. "The feeling's mutual, darlin'."

That wasn't exactly a surprise—and *darlin'* wasn't a term of endearment—but Eden had had no choice about what she'd done. If she hadn't come here, the man behind this would have no doubt just sent someone else. Someone who would have gone through with the job, leaving her in danger with the militia groups.

"And I came out here because I thought I could help," she added. "I didn't think it was fair for me to be tucked away inside while you fought this fight for me."

He made another of those sarcastic sounds. "I'm not doing it for you. Might not have noticed, but they're shooting at me, too. And my brother. That makes this my fight." And he fired another shot.

The gunman retaliated. His next shot smacked into the corner of the house, causing Declan to curse and haul her closer to him. He practically climbed on top of her, shielding her with his body. It was his training that'd kicked in, no doubt, because after everything that'd just gone on inside his house, there's no way he'd truly want to protect her.

Unless it was just so he could interrogate her.

Yes, that had to be it.

He'd want the truth. Heck, so did she, and he wasn't going to be pleased when he realized she didn't have it. First, though, they had to survive this, and the way the bullets were coming at them, that might not happen.

The new position with Declan was far from comfortable. Her pressed against the icy ground. Him pressed against her. Every muscle in his body was tight and primed.

The shooter in the tree fired more shots, but in the mix of those battering sounds, Eden heard a different shot. Declan no doubt heard it as well, because his attention shifted from the front to the back. He didn't fire. He just lay there, waiting.

It didn't take long for Eden to realize the gunman at the back of the property was no longer firing. Unlike the tree shooter. That guy picked up the pace, the shots coming at them nonstop.

Declan and she needed to move, since the bullets were tearing their way through the side of the house. Soon the wooden planks wouldn't provide any cover for them at all. But they probably shouldn't move onto the porch, not with the other gunman still out back.

Except he wasn't shooting.

No one back there was.

Still, Declan didn't budge. Didn't return fire, either. Maybe because he was running low on ammunition.

His phone buzzed, and without taking his attention off the gunman, Declan pressed the button to answer it. He didn't put the call on speaker, but Eden was close enough to hear his brother Wyatt.

"The gunman back here is down," Wyatt said. "I'm moving closer to check and see if he's alive. Don't think he is, though."

Declan clipped off most of the groan that left his mouth. "Get to him fast, and if there's an ounce of breath left in him, make him talk. I'm moving my *visitor* back inside."

And that was exactly what Declan started to do the moment he ended the call. He fired a shot at the gunman, hauled Eden to her feet and they scrambled across the porch and back into the house. Once they were inside, he pointed to the sofa.

"Get behind that and stay there," Declan ordered, and there was no mistaking that it was an order. He hurried back to the window, the broken glass crunching beneath his boots.

Eden did get behind the sofa, but she hated that Declan was the one taking the risks here. They were in this mess together, and she only wished she'd been able to figure out a way to diffuse this before it had ever started.

She thought of her sisters. Of the danger they were in, too. They didn't deserve this. Neither did she. The sins of the father were coming at them with a vengeance.

Maybe.

And maybe this had more to do with Declan.

Maybe this had nothing to do with her at all. Or her father. Maybe there was some other connection between Declan and her that she'd missed. Once they were out of this, she had to beef up security for her sisters and do some more digging, because there were a lot of unanswered questions.

"Hell," Declan grumbled. He fired out the gaping holes in the window where there'd once been glass. And he cursed again. He shot her a glance from over his shoulder. "Stay here, and this time you'd better do it."

Eden shook her head. "You're not going back out there."

"The gunman's getting away."

No, that couldn't happen. Especially if the other gunman was dead. They needed this one alive so they could question him and learn who'd hired him to do this. And why. If he got away, Eden figured it wouldn't be the end of it. The guy's boss would just regroup and launch another attack. And this time, she might not be able to protect her family.

Still, she didn't want Declan shot, or worse.

She was about to offer backup again, which she knew he'd refuse, but Eden didn't even get to make the offer. Declan ran out of the room, and a moment later she heard him leave through the back door.

Eden held her breath and tried to pick through the sounds around her—the ticking clock on the mantel, the wind outside, her own body shivering from the cold that was pouring in through the window—and she heard footsteps on the back porch. In case it wasn't Declan, she turned in that direction. Aimed her gun. And tried to brace herself for whatever might happen.

It was entirely possible that the gunman wasn't getting away at all but would backtrack and come through that front door. She knew for a fact that it wasn't locked. Neither door had been when she'd arrived at the place earlier. Obviously, Declan hadn't been concerned about security.

He would be now.

If he survived this, that is.

The sound of the shot blasting through the air caused her fear to spike. She was pretty sure it hadn't come from Declan's gun but rather their attacker's. And it sounded close. That meant the man likely hadn't escaped after all, that instead he'd just changed positions so that he could ambush Declan.

"You okay, Declan?" someone shouted. Probably Wyatt.

Declan didn't answer, and that didn't help the fear roaring through her. Despite his order for her to stay put, Eden stayed crouched down, but she made her way to the window. It took her several heart-stopping moments before she caught just a glimpse of Declan. He peered around the edge of the house before he snapped back out of sight.

For a good reason.

Another shot. This one took out a chunk of the house right where Declan was.

Eden got her gun ready, and her gaze fired all around in an effort to see what she could of the house and grounds. She still didn't see the shooter, but judging from the angle of that last shot, he was somewhere near Declan's black truck. It was certainly large enough to conceal a man and give him decent cover, but the guy might also use it to escape.

She caught some movement from the corner of her eye. Not Declan. Not by the truck, either. This was on the other side of the yard near a cluster of cottonwoods with their winter-bare branches. Someone was behind the trunk of the largest tree, and even though she only got a glimpse of him, she thought it might be Wyatt. She hoped so anyway.

The shots stopped, and quiet settled in. Declan didn't come out from cover. Neither did the shooter or the other man behind the cottonwood. The deafening shots had been bad enough, but the silence allowed her to think, and the only thing she could think about was just how deadly this had turned and how much worse it could get.

And then the silence shattered.

Declan shouted something, and he bolted out from the side of the house. Not standing up, either. He was on the ground and slid forward on the ice-crusted grass. Aiming low, he fired.

On the other side of the yard, the man behind the cottonwood did the same.

Both shots went in the direction of the truck. But not through it, beneath it. She heard the gunman howl in pain.

"Drop your weapon!" Declan shouted. He got to his feet and, using the trees for cover, he made his way closer to the truck.

It seemed to take an eternity, but the gunman finally limped out while he held on to the truck. Probably because, from what she could tell, he'd been shot in his lower left leg and upper right thigh. He threw his rifle onto the ground and lifted his left hand in the air.

"I need a doctor, quick." The gunman's voice was a hoarse growl and didn't mask the pain.

His injuries didn't seem to be life threatening, but he was bleeding. Eden didn't have much sympathy for someone who'd just tried to kill them, but she wanted him alive. And talking.

The gunman was wearing dark clothes and a stocking cap, but she could see his face now. He was heavily muscled and had a wide nose that appeared to have been broken a couple of times. Part of her had hoped she might recognize him. A former disgruntled client, maybe. Or someone associated with her father. But no. He was a stranger.

"Call an ambulance," Declan instructed Wyatt.

His brother stepped fully out from the cottonwood and took out his phone.

"Why are you here?" Declan asked the man. He kept his gun trained on him and walked closer.

"I'm on orders." The man caught onto the truck with both hands, and that answer seemed to take a lot of effort. But at least now they knew he was a hired gun.

Well, unless he was lying.

Declan inched closer to the man. Wyatt, too, after he put his phone back in his pocket.

"The ambulance is on the way," Wyatt relayed. "But my advice is for you to start talking."

The man glanced around as if trying to figure out what to do. She prayed he didn't try to pick up his gun and attempt an escape. It'd be suicide with two armed marshals closing in on him.

"Talking wouldn't be good for my health," he answered. "Call that ambulance and tell them to hurry up."

Wyatt didn't make an attempt to do that. Both Declan and he moved forward, both still using the trees as cover until they reached the clearing between the truck and them. The gunman didn't appear to have any other weapons, but maybe Declan and Wyatt would stay put until the ambulance arrived. The thought had no sooner crossed her mind than she heard the sound.

Another blast.

Definitely a gunshot, but this one seemed to come out of nowhere. Eden shouted for Declan and his brother to get down, but her warning wasn't necessary. They were already headed to the ground anyway, but they hadn't managed to do that before there was another shot.

Then another.

Eden sucked in her breath hard, and with her gun gripped in her hand, she pivoted from one side to the other, bracing herself to see the shots slam into either Declan or Wyatt. Or both.

But that didn't happen.

The gunman by the truck lurched forward, the impact of the bullets jolting through his body. It all happened in a split second, but he crumpled into a heap on the ground.

"Someone shot him," she mumbled. And that someone wasn't Declan or his brother.

"Who the hell fired those shots?" Declan asked.

But Wyatt only shook his head. "Not the guy in the back, because he's dead. I had to shoot him."

Eden got ready to return fire. Wyatt and Declan did the same, but there were no more shots. In fact, there was no sign of the person who'd just shot the gunman.

But there was another sound.

The roar of a car engine. It was on the west side of the property. Probably on the old ranch trail. Eden knew it was there because that was where she'd left her own vehicle.

"He's getting away!" Declan shouted, and he raced in the direction of the sound.

That brought Eden back onto the porch, and she eased out into the yard, following Wyatt.

Toward the downed gunman.

Wyatt made it to the man first, and he stooped down, put his fingers to the man's neck. Because of the angle of his face, Eden couldn't see his expression, but she got a clear view of Declan's when he started running back toward them.

Declan kept watch behind him, but he took out his phone and requested assistance. The ranch trail led to the main road, and he asked for someone to respond to that area immediately. He didn't stop there. He hauled her behind the truck. Probably because he didn't want her out in the open in case that gunman returned.

Wyatt met his brother's gaze before he moved away from the man on the ground. "He's dead."

Declan mumbled something she didn't catch, but she didn't need to hear it to see the frustration in his eyes and face. "You're sure the other gunman is dead, too?"

Wyatt nodded. "There was no ID on him. Nothing except extra ammo...and a note."

That snagged both Declan's and her attention. "What kind of note?" Declan asked.

Eden figured that whatever it was, it couldn't be good. Hired killers didn't usually bring happy news.

"It's a single sheet of paper, folded. It was sticking out of the guy's pocket, but I looked at it when I saw Kirby's name scrawled on the outside."

"Why would a hired gun have a note addressed to your father?" she asked at the same time Declan asked, "What did the note say?"

Wyatt pulled in a long breath. "It didn't make sense. It said something like, 'This is just the beginning. You can't save him.'"

Declan shook his head. "Who's *him?*"

Wyatt met his gaze. "*You,* Declan."

Chapter Five

Declan slipped on the latex gloves that he'd taken from his equipment bag at his house, stooped down and pulled the note from the dead man's pocket. Yeah, it was addressed to Kirby all right.

"Is it really a death threat?" Eden asked. She was right behind him, peering over his shoulder. And she was shaking. Not just her voice, her whole body was trembling.

He figured Wyatt hadn't gotten the contents of the message wrong, but Declan had to see it for himself. There wasn't much to read.

This is just the beginning, Kirby Granger. You can't save him. O'Malley's a dead man.

It'd been handwritten almost in a childish scrawl with green crayon. Maybe as an attempt to disguise any handwriting characteristics. But Declan would have it analyzed anyway. He slipped it into a plastic evidence bag.

"Why does someone want you dead?" Eden asked.

She'd only been around him for the past couple of hours, and she'd already asked him that several times. Too bad it was a question he didn't have an answer for.

He stood and started back toward his house, where

the chaos was in full swing. A different kind of chaos from the attack. The crime-scene folks had arrived. Two of his brothers, Dallas and Slade. Sheriff Rico Geary and his deputies, too. It wasn't exactly a local case what with the attempted murder of two federal marshals, but Geary had people in place to preserve the crime scene. Plus, the sheriff wouldn't do anything to keep Declan and his brothers out of any part of this investigation.

Not that he could have anyway.

Declan wasn't sure what'd happened here, but he would find out, one way or another. Apparently, Eden had the same idea, because she'd been on and off her phone since the attack. All of this was just for starters. Declan wanted to question Eden a lot more so he could try to pinpoint the person who'd set all of this in motion.

Maybe she knew.

Maybe she didn't.

He was leaning toward *didn't* since she'd nearly been killed. Most people didn't protect a person who wanted them dead. And besides, she was genuinely worried about her two sisters, since most of her calls had centered on arranging extra protection for them. Declan would add his own layer of protection soon by calling the marshals in that area.

"This is connected to your foster father," Eden said, falling into step beside him. "The note proves that."

"No. The note proves nothing. Someone could have written it to muddy the waters."

She made a slight sound of surprise, then frustration. Maybe because she hadn't thought of that angle first. Still, Declan couldn't take his muddy-water theory as gospel, and that meant talking to Kirby. Maybe there was something that connected all three of them— Eden, Kirby and him. Something linked to the photo of him and his family back in Germany. And Declan had a sickening feeling that it was a connection he wasn't going to like.

"Thank you," she said in a hoarse whisper. "For saving my life."

Declan just gave a noncommittal grunt. He couldn't issue a standard "you're welcome" without choking on it, because he'd told her to stay put and she hadn't.

Yeah, she was hardheaded all right. And up to her pretty neck in danger. A real bad combination. She had just enough guts and skills to get herself killed. Him, too, since his stupid body had decided to protect her. But then, protecting her was the only way to get those answers.

When they reached the front of his house, he saw the medical examiner's crew loading the dead gunman into their van. The guy had the two gunshot wounds to the legs that Wyatt and he had given him. But it was the gaping hole in the back of his head that'd done him in.

"Not an amateur's shot," Declan mumbled.

Wyatt nodded in agreement and pointed to the woods directly ahead. They were thick and dark despite the lack of leaves. "Dallas and Slade are down there having a look around."

Because it was probably where a rifleman had positioned himself to kill the gunman.

A hit man for the hit man.

Sometimes, karma worked. But in this case, it hadn't worked in Declan's favor.

"Any sign of the shooter?" Eden asked.

"None." Wyatt clearly wasn't happy about that, either. Neither was Declan. But they'd gotten someone out to the area as fast as possible and had simply missed the guy. Of course, if he was a pro, and Declan was pretty sure he was, then he would have had his escape route well planned out.

"There are some tire tracks," Wyatt went on. "We'll do castings of those."

It was all standard procedure, but standard didn't seem like nearly enough.

"Maybe we're dealing with two factions here," Eden said. "Someone's trying to kill Declan and someone else is trying to protect him."

"Or someone didn't want the gunman to talk," Wyatt supplied.

Declan was leaning toward that theory. And it meant the person behind this really didn't want his or her identity revealed and wasn't willing to risk a hired gun running his mouth.

"I'll do mop-up," Wyatt assured him, and the sheriff added his nod to that. Wyatt motioned for Declan to hand him the evidence bag with the note inside.

Declan hated to leave his brothers with the chore of processing a crime scene this big, and this personal, but there were other things that needed to be done. Plus, Eden's trembling was getting worse with every passing second, and soon the adrenaline crash would hit her hard. Him, too. But at least he had some experience dealing with it. He was betting she didn't.

"Come on," Declan insisted.

But Eden held her ground when he tried to help her into the truck. "My car's on the back trail, and I need to leave to check on my sisters."

He looked her straight in the eye. "And what happens if the gunman comes after you when you're with them, huh?"

She flinched, then quickly recovered. "The gunman will more likely come after you."

"After *us*," he corrected. "For whatever reason, someone involved you in this, and you're not leaving my sight until I find out why. There's also the part about you coming here to pretend to kill me."

She budged, but after he practically pushed her into the cab of his truck. "You think I'm lying about being blackmailed into doing this?"

Declan shrugged, got in and drove away. "Not lying exactly, but maybe not telling me the whole truth."

"I don't know the whole truth," she practically shouted. She groaned, a sound of pure frustration, and she yanked on her seat belt. "I just know I don't want to be involved with this. Or with you."

She stumbled over the last word, causing Declan to glance at her. There was just another of those disturbing split-second glances where he saw the unguarded expression in those baby blues. There was fear in her eyes. But something else.

Great.

It was the kind of look a woman gave a man. Not one she was hired to kill, either. It was a look that smacked of attraction, and it made Declan curse.

Because he was feeling it, too.

As soon as he figured out how, he was going to make it go away. He didn't need the kind of trouble that Eden Gray brought with her. Especially since he'd been the one to arrest her father. Even though she didn't appear to be holding any grudges about that, maybe those blue eyes were concealing things well hidden.

She looked away from him. "Where are you taking me?"

"Since the EMTs are going to be tied up with the gunmen for a while, first stop is the hospital. You should be checked out by the doctor, and Kirby's there. He was a little weak after his last cancer treatment, and they decided to keep him a day or two."

"I'm sorry. How sick is he?"

"Sick," Declan settled for saying, and it was all he intended to say on the matter. Kirby could be dying, and there was nothing he could do about it.

"Maybe questioning him is a bad idea then," she added.

Yeah, it was. Kirby didn't need this while he was trying to recover, but there was no way to keep the news of the gunfight from him. Even while he was in the hospital. Someone would let it slip, and Kirby would be furious that he hadn't heard it from Declan. Besides, Kirby might be able to shed some light on the note.

"I don't need to see a doctor," she said. She reached out and touched his chin. "But you should."

Declan hadn't been expecting that touch, and he actually flinched. First, from the contact. Then the little zing of pain as her fingers grazed his skin. When Eden drew back her fingers, he saw the blood.

"You might need stitches," she suggested.

He jerked down the visor with the vanity mirror and had a look. Yeah, his chin was cut all right, but there was no way he'd take the time to get stitches. He reached over to the glove compartment, the back of his hand brushing against Eden's jeans-clad leg, and this time she was the one who flinched.

"Good grief," she mumbled. "What's wrong with us?"

Oh, she knew what.

So did he.

"My advice?" He took some tissues from the glove compartment and pressed them against his chin. "Pretend it's not there." Since she didn't question what *it* was, he figured they were on the same page.

Talk about lousy timing.

And bad judgment.

Of course, that idiot part of him behind his jeans' zipper was a bad-judgment magnet. He had a way of hooking up with women who could give him the most amount of trouble in the least amount of time.

The most fun, too.

Still, this went beyond his fondness for bad girls whose middles names were Trouble. Because this bad girl had been sent to kill him.

"Any chance your father's behind this?" Declan came right out and asked. He expected her to have a quick denial and figured she wouldn't admit that Zander Gray would try to kill his own daughter.

"There's no way he would put me at risk like this." She paused. "But he hates you. A lot. And he blames you for his arrest."

"He should blame himself. He's the one who tried to murder a witness."

"He said he was innocent and I believe him."

Not exactly a surprise. "Well, I'm just as adamant that he's as guilty as sin." Declan took the final turn toward town. "Would he include you in any plan to get revenge against me?"

He looked for any signs that she'd been lying, that she'd been in on this plan from the beginning—all to help her father get back at him.

"No." There was just a slight hesitation before she repeated it.

Maybe she wasn't as certain as she wanted to seem. Declan sure wasn't, and her father gave them a starting point. But before trying to track down the man who'd been a fugitive for months, he needed to deal with the note.

Well, maybe.

It was possible that Kirby would be too weak to talk. Still, he could at least have Eden checked out to make sure she was okay. He didn't see any cuts or bruises, but she'd hit the ground pretty hard when he had dragged her off the porch and away from those bullets.

He pulled into the parking lot of the hospital and looked around to make sure they hadn't been followed. Something he'd done on the entire drive. The missing gunman probably wouldn't choose Main Street for an attack, but Declan didn't want to take any chances.

"This way." He led Eden through a side door for one of the clinics located in the hospital. It was an entrance he and his brothers had been using a lot lately so they wouldn't have to go through the newly installed metal detectors and disarm. With Kirby's frequent stays in the hospital, it saved all of them some time.

Declan wound through the maze of corridors, and when he got to the wing with Kirby's room, he spotted his brother Harlan in the hall. He was pacing and talking on the phone, but he ended the call when he saw Declan.

"My brother, Marshal Harlan McKinney," Declan said, making introductions. "And this is Eden Gray."

"Yeah. I just did a background check on her." Harlan stared at her. Nope, glared. "She's a P.I. all right, but she's also—"

"Zander Gray's daughter," she finished for him. She extended her hand, waited, until Harlan shook it. His brother was intimidating with his linebacker-size shoulders and dark, edgy looks, but Eden didn't back down. Maybe because she'd already faced worse today. Even Harlan wasn't worse than flying bullets.

Harlan's gaze shifted to Declan, and he took out his phone to scroll through what was on the screen. "She's twenty-nine, single, owns the Gray Agency, but she's the only full-time employee. Last night, she went to the prison to visit her father's former cellmate."

Now it was Declan's turn to glare at her.

"I didn't speak to him," Eden quickly explained. "He refused to see me. But I wanted to ask him if he knew my father's whereabouts. I wanted to find out if my father knew anything about the bogus info planted on my computer."

Since Harlan likely didn't know anything about that yet, Declan finished the explanation for her. "We need to get a tech into her computer system."

She was shaking her head before he even finished. "If you do that, the info will be leaked, and it'll cause the two opposing militia factions to come after me."

Harlan looked at him to no doubt see if he was buying this. Unfortunately, he was. It wasn't that hard to hack into a computer, plant info and change the password. It wasn't that hard to rile militia groups, either. But the problem was that still didn't give them answers about who was behind this and why. It was a lot of effort, and it'd taken money to hire a computer hacker, the photographer who'd gobbled up those pictures of him and the three gunmen.

"I need to talk to Kirby about the note on the dead gunman," Declan said. Yeah, he was avoiding any further discussion about Eden's innocence—or lack thereof—so he could move on to something that had to be done.

Harlan nodded eventually. But Declan could tell his brother didn't approve. None of them wanted to do anything to make Kirby's situation worse, and this might qualify as worse.

"And I'll see what I can do about getting the info erased from her computer," Harlan offered.

"Thanks. Could you also take Eden to Dr. Landry so she can be checked out?"

"Eden?" Harlan obviously didn't like Declan's use of her given name, either.

But Eden clearly didn't like the checkup suggestion. "I want to hear what your foster father has to say."

Declan would have given her a firm no, but the door to Kirby's room opened and Stella Doyle stepped out. She was a fixture around Kirby these days.

"I heard voices," Stella said, and her attention zoomed in on the cut on Declan's chin. "Are you all right? Were you hurt?" And that concern extended to Eden when Stella's gaze shifted in her direction.

"We're fine," Declan lied. As he'd done with Harlan, he made introductions.

"You worked at the Rocky Creek Children's Facility," Eden said to Stella. "I read through everything I could find about you, and the others."

"I did work there," Stella confirmed. "A bad place. Bad times, too."

Harlan's phone buzzed and he stepped to the side to take the call. A moment later, he took out a small notepad from his pocket and started writing.

Stella glanced behind her at Kirby. Declan glanced, too, and didn't like what he saw. Kirby was hooked up to several machines, and he seemed paler than he had been lately. And he'd been pretty darn pale. His eyes were also closed, and his breathing was shallow.

"How is he?" Declan asked.

Stella studied his expression. Then Eden's. "Not strong enough for bad news. Is that what you brought with you?"

"Maybe. There was a note addressed to Kirby in the dead hit man's pocket. It said 'This is just the beginning,

Kirby Granger. You can't save him. O'Malley's a dead man.' I need to ask Kirby if he knows what it means."

Stella's hand moved to her mouth, but he still heard the sharp gasp she made, and her eyes widened. For just a second. Then she cleared her throat. But Declan didn't think it was his imagination that she was fighting to hang on to her composure along with something she didn't want him to know.

Hell.

He was tired of people keeping things from him. First Eden. Now, apparently, Stella.

"Who wrote that?" Stella demanded. She stepped out into the hall and shut Kirby's door.

Declan shook his head. "I don't know. That's why we're here."

"You can't ask him." Stella said it so fast that her words ran together, but then her demand came to a grinding halt. "If Kirby were to find out that someone wants you dead, it might break him. He's barely hanging on now, Declan. Fighting, yes. But I don't have to tell you that it's a fight he might lose."

No, she didn't have to tell him. That fear was always there, not on the back burner but rather in the front of his mind. However, he still had the feeling that Stella wasn't telling him everything.

But what?

He trusted her. Well, for the most part. He had yet to rule her out as a suspect in Jonah Webb's murder. All of them had motive, since Webb was physically abusing Declan and plenty of the other kids. And with Stella working there and seeing the abuse, she might have helped Webb's wife murder him and hide the body.

Of course, Kirby could have done it, too.

Or any of his brothers.

Still, Declan wasn't about to press them on that subject. Webb had deserved everything he got, and if Stella had helped deliver the fatal blow, then he wasn't going to be the one to arrest her.

"When Kirby wakes up," Stella said, her voice a little uneven, "I'll tell him about the note. But I'll leave out the part about your being a dead man."

"Thanks."

Even though it was the best they could do right now, Eden looked as if she wanted to press matters. She volleyed her attention between Stella, him and the door to Kirby's room. But she finally just huffed and dropped back a step.

"You look tuckered out," Stella said, giving Eden's arm a gentle rub. "Why don't you have Declan take you somewhere so you can get some rest."

Eden shook her head. "Thanks, but I don't want to rest."

Yeah, but Declan figured she needed it. After the hellish morning they'd had, they both needed it, but getting it probably wouldn't happen.

"Who's at the ranch?" Declan asked.

"None of the family," Stella answered. "Everyone's either tied up with the shooting or with other work. Lenora, Joelle, Caitlyn and Maya all went to San Antonio for a big Christmas-shopping trip. They took the babies with them. Won't be back until sometime tomorrow."

His sisters-in-law and three nephews. And it was good that they weren't at the ranch, since that was where he might eventually take Eden to regroup and try to figure out who'd put that information on her computer. That was the starting point anyway.

"I should go back in with Kirby," Stella added. "I'll

let you know what he says when I can ask him about the note."

Declan nodded, thanked her. Her offer seemed right, but there was something a little off with the tone of her voice. Maybe because she dreaded telling Kirby about the attack. And she would have to tell him. It didn't matter how little info Stella gave him, Kirby would piece it together, and he would demand to know everything that was going on.

Harlan finished his call, and before he made his way back to them, Declan knew something was wrong. Harlan always wore a bad-news expression, but it was even worse now.

His brother pulled in a long breath. "First, the FBI techs used remote access from Quantico and managed to get the planted information off Eden's computer. Well, actually, they confiscated everything on the hard drive and server so it can't be leaked."

That was better than good news. They darn sure didn't need the militia groups adding more danger to this already dangerous mess.

"They managed to do that fast," Eden said, shaking her head. "If I'd called them first—"

"These men would have just hired someone else to come after me," Declan interrupted. Besides, he didn't want the FBI involved other than to erase the computer info. Not with so many clues pointing right back to Kirby.

And possibly the Webb murder.

"And what's the bad news?" Declan asked his brother.

Harlan didn't deny there was some, and his mumbled profanity confirmed it. "We have the identities of the two dead gunmen. Howard Starling and Neil Packard."

Declan looked at Eden, but she only shook her head. "I don't recognize either name. Who are they?"

"Hired muscle." Harlan looked at his notes. "And they've worked for a variety of criminals in high and low places."

"Anyone we know?" Declan asked.

"Yeah." He turned the note for them to read. There were nearly a dozen names on the list, but Harlan tapped the last one. "But I think you'll agree that this is the man who hired them to kill you."

Chapter Six

Eden braced herself for the name of the person that Harlan was pointing out to them, but when she saw it, she had to groan. "Leonard Kane."

Unfortunately, it was someone she recognized. And one she didn't want on that list because it was a connection that led right back to her.

"He was your father's former business partner," Harlan said, and it sounded like some kind of accusation against her. Declan didn't echo the accusation, but he did stare at her, and he obviously wanted yet more information that she just didn't have.

"My father had a lot of business partners," she explained. "And besides, Leonard and he had a major falling-out years ago. Long before you arrested him and his escape from jail. Leonard believes my father backstabbed him on a business deal, one that ended up costing Leonard a great deal of money."

Declan's stare didn't let up one bit. "Rifts can be mended, and they could have teamed up to put together that attack today."

But that didn't make sense.

"Why come after us now?" she asked. "I mean, Declan arrested my father over three years ago. Why wait all this time to settle old scores? And why include me in any part of it? I didn't have anything to do with those business dealings."

"Maybe Leonard didn't have the resources in place three years ago to do this," Declan readily answered. Then he shook his head. "But it feels like more than that. If the idea is to get even with both of us, why not just shoot and kill us?"

That sent a shiver through her. It wasn't exactly a comforting thought that someone could have put a bullet in her at any time. Declan, too. After all, those pictures someone had taken of him could have been a gunman firing bullets. But while there was bad blood between Declan and her father—Declan and her, too—her father wouldn't do this.

Leonard was another matter.

"Maybe this is Leonard's way of getting back at my father. He could be trying to torment us," she suggested. "A cat-and-mouse game."

"But the game could have ended today with those shots," Harlan pointed out.

Declan shook his head again. "I'm not sure the attack was supposed to go down like that. Maybe that's why someone took out the shooter."

It made sense. Well, as much sense as this whole puzzling situation could make. But if the intent was only to torment them, why link Declan and her together? The torment could have happened without hacking into her computer and blackmailing her into attempted murder.

"I'll see about getting Leonard in for questioning," Harlan volunteered. "I can run a deep background check, too. What about Dr. Landry? You still want her to check out Eden?" He said her name with slightly less disdain this time. Perhaps because Declan's brother was beginning to believe she was innocent in all of this.

And Eden prayed she was.

She hadn't done anything intentionally to make this happen, but the connection to Leonard and her father was just plain unnerving. Especially since Leonard hated her father and vice versa.

"I don't want to see the doctor," Eden insisted. She had much more important things to do, so she took out her phone. "I do want to check on my sisters, though. And my car, which I left near Declan's."

"I'll arrange to have the car brought to the ranch," Declan told her. "After it's been checked for bugs and tracking devices."

It was a good idea, and something she wished she'd thought of. Her mind was so fuzzy now. Definitely not what she needed, because a fuzzy head could get her killed. Declan, too.

"And as for talking to your sisters, don't use your cell," Declan went on. "If the hacker was skilled enough to get into your computer, he could just as easily trace your phone. It's probably not a good idea for that missing gunman to be able to keep tabs on you."

Something else she hadn't considered but should have.

"I'll have someone check on the security arrangements for her sisters," Harlan continued. He glanced at the exit. "Best if you two don't hang around here much longer."

Because the gunman could track them there. If that was indeed what the missing man wanted to do. But something else occurred to her. If the gunman did track them here to the hospital, then it could put other members of Declan's foster family in danger. She didn't want that. There'd already been enough danger for one day.

"I'll take Eden to the marshals' office so we can make

our statements about the shooting." Declan looked at her. "After that, we'll go to the ranch."

"No," she immediately protested. "No need to take this fight there."

"It's the safest place to take it." But then Declan shrugged. "Maybe. I guess that depends on what we learn in the next couple of hours."

Yes, and she prayed there wouldn't be another attack on them or on anyone else. But she had a horrible feeling that the attacks would just continue until they stopped the person behind them.

"I'll keep you posted on whatever I get," Harlan added, and Declan led her back down the hall and out the side door where they'd entered.

The blast of cold hit her the moment they stepped outside, and Eden started shivering. By the time they'd made it across the parking lot to his truck, she was past the shivering stage, and her teeth were chattering.

"It's the adrenaline crash," Declan said, and he turned the heater on full blast. He also looked around. One of those sweeping glances that cops did when they were making sure everything was safe.

Of course, everything wasn't safe.

The realization of that hit her hard, and the sound of those gunshots started to roar through her head. That didn't help the shivering, either. "Just give me a second. I don't want to go into the marshals' building like this."

"Everybody there has seen worse." Declan rummaged behind his seat and came up with a plaid wool blanket. "It's probably been on the horses, but at least it'll keep you warm. Or not," he added when she just kept shaking.

She hugged the blanket to her. Yes, it'd been on the horses. She didn't mind the scent, but the extra layer of warmth still gave her no relief. Even worse, her eyes started to water.

Good grief.

She didn't need this. Neither did Declan. Falling apart would only make things worse.

"Hell," he said under his breath, and he hooked his arm around her and dragged her closer to him. "There's a middle seat belt. Use it."

She did, somehow managing to get it on while Declan drove out of the hospital parking lot. He kept his arm around her. Kept her close, too. Shoulder to shoulder and so snug against him that she caught his scent. Not the horse scent on the blanket, but Declan's. It sent a trickle of heat through her that her body welcomed but she certainly didn't.

Because that heat was a huge problem.

He glanced at her. Frowned. "Now you're breathing too fast and your face is flushed. If this keeps up, I'm turning around and taking you back to see the doctor."

"You're causing the fast breath." She kept her voice at a whisper, but he heard her anyway.

His frown got worse. His eyes narrowed a bit. "I think we can both agree that nothing should happen between us."

She nodded. But that *should* was still lingering in the air between them. The heat from the attraction, too.

"I don't have sex with women like you," he added. Then cursed. "That's a lie. You're exactly the kind I take to my bed."

Her breathing went from fast to warp speed. That wasn't the right thing to admit to her. Especially not now. "It doesn't matter that I'm your usual type, because I'm still the wrong woman."

"You got it." He flashed a half smile that melted the

ball of ice in her stomach. "But then, I'm the wrong man for you." No half smile now. "And I'm pretty sure in a stupid-sex world, that makes this one of those irresistible situations we're just going to have to resist. Or at least keep reminding ourselves to resist."

Yes. She wondered, though, if a reminder would be just a waste of mental energy. "I don't want to find you attractive." But she did. Mercy, did she. On a scale of one to ten, he was a six hundred, and even with the danger, he fired every nerve in her body.

"Ditto," he snarled. "Don't want it, but you are. In fact, you've got those bad-girl eyes."

She frowned. "They're blue."

"They're bedroom eyes. But it's not the eyes that have me cursing. It's the rest of you." He glanced down to where they made contact. Specifically at the way her breast was right against his chest.

"Yes," she agreed. Even though it was something she should keep to herself, she didn't. "The rest of you is causing problems for me, too."

And that was why Eden leaned away from him. She instantly felt the loss of warmth from his body, but she kept the inch or so of space between them.

Declan didn't say another word, and didn't move her back toward him, either, thank goodness. He just drove down Main Street until he turned into the parking lot of the marshals' building. He looked around again, and Eden ditched the blanket before they hurried inside.

Bedroom eyes, indeed. Better than his bedroom body. And she pushed that uneasy thought and images aside so she could face what would no doubt be another ordeal.

They went through security and reception, then up the stairs to a maze of office cubicles and desks. The moment they stepped inside, Declan's attention zoomed across the room to a tall, lanky marshal who was on the phone. She recognized him as Marshal Dallas Walker, Declan's foster brother. He held his finger up in a wait-a-second gesture and then quickly ended the call.

"Please tell me someone caught the gunman," Declan said.

But Dallas only shook his head. "No gunman, but I just got an earful on our suspect, Leonard Kane." He stopped, looked at her. "Zander Gray's daughter, huh."

Not a question, and he didn't wait for her to confirm it. Eden could tell from his brusque tone that here was yet another foster brother who didn't like her. Or trust her.

"What about Leonard?" Declan prompted when his brother's glare lingered on her.

Dallas's gaze came back to Declan. "Over thirty years ago Kirby shot and killed Leonard's son, Corey, when he was evading arrest. Leonard vowed revenge and said he'd make Kirby pay by killing a son of his." Dallas looked at her again as if he expected her to have more information.

She didn't. "This is the first I'm hearing about this. But then, I haven't had any reason to dig into Leonard's background. Well, not before now anyway."

If either of them believed her, there was no sign of it in their expressions.

"Over thirty years ago?" Declan asked. "That's a long time to hold off on taking revenge."

"Yeah," Dallas agreed. "Leonard just got some bad news. He's dying. And not like Kirby's cancer. This is an inoperable brain tumor. He's got less than six months, and according to a criminal informant, Leonard's been cleaning house and tying up old loose ends. One of his former business partners was found dead a week ago."

Eden's stomach knotted. The news just kept getting worse. "Any way to link it to Leonard?"

"None so far. The man has plenty of money to cover his tracks." Wyatt paused. "I think Leonard's threat is clear, though, about going after Kirby's son."

"But he has six foster sons," Eden pointed out.

"Technically, Kirby has just five. He had to adopt one because of some legal technicalities that had to do with all that mess that happened at the Rocky Creek Children's Facility."

"Which one?

"Me," Declan answered.

He didn't add anything else, but it was clear to Eden that there was something to add. She didn't like these secrets, whatever they were, but they had bigger fish to fry, and that fish's name was Leonard Kane.

"So Leonard wanted me to kill Declan to get back at Kirby," she concluded.

Dallas lifted his shoulder. "With your father, Zander, either dead or unwilling to surface, it's my guess that Leonard will want to take his revenge out on you."

That ice knot in her stomach returned with a vengeance. "Me?"

Dallas held up his phone for her to see. "The CSI found this on the windshield of your car."

Both Declan and she leaned in, their attention zooming to the photo of the message. It was short but definitely not sweet.

Your life for hers, Zander. Time's running out.

Chapter Seven

Declan downed the rest of his coffee and poured himself another cup. It was strong, but he wished it were a whole lot stronger. Because he was no doubt going to need it to get through this day.

"That was the crime lab," Wyatt said the moment he finished his latest call. He was at the kitchen table at the ranch with Declan, both of them with laptops in front of them while they read over reports and updates on the attack. "The only prints on the threatening notes were those of the dead gunmen."

It was exactly what Declan had expected. This had been a well-planned attack, and the person who'd orchestrated it wouldn't have wanted to leave incriminating evidence behind. Well, unless it incriminated the wrong person.

Is that what'd happened with the note left on Eden's car?

Your life for hers, Zander. Time's running out.

Even though it seemed to be a challenge for Zander, he could have written it himself to throw them off his trail. If there was a trail, that is. Even with all the resources of the FBI and the Marshals' Service, they hadn't been able to find hide nor hair of the man.

"No sign of the missing gunman," Wyatt added,

"though they're running the tire tracks to see if they can come up with a vehicle match."

They might get lucky. *Might.* But he figured they'd need more than luck to break this case.

Declan heard the sound of someone moving around upstairs. Eden, no doubt, since he'd given the housekeeper the day off. And with Stella and Kirby at the hospital and his sisters-in-law on their extended Christmas-shopping trip, Wyatt, Eden and he had the place to themselves. Best if it stayed that way for a while.

If he could convince Eden, that is.

She hadn't exactly been thrilled that he'd taken her to the ranch for the night, but after they'd given their statements about the shooting, she'd been past the point of exhaustion. And the bottom line was, the ranch had a decent security system and was well guarded by the ranch hands who knew how to use a gun.

"What are you going to do about her?" Wyatt asked, his attention drifting to the footsteps they could now hear on the stairs.

"Not sure." In fact, Declan wasn't sure of anything when it came to Eden, except that she seemed to be in as much danger as he was. Even if she hadn't been the target of yesterday's attack, those bullets could have killed her.

"You trust her?" his brother pressed.

"No." But then he stopped. Rethought it.

Hell. Yes, he did.

He didn't want to trust her, but apparently that whole damsel-in-distress, bedroom-eyes thing was playing into this. As was the attraction. He reminded himself that attraction shouldn't equal trust. But it might take another bullet or two for that to sink in.

Eden hurried into the kitchen. Practically running.

And she also practically skidded to a stop when her gaze landed on Wyatt. Maybe because Wyatt was glaring at her again.

"Sorry," she mumbled. "I didn't mean to sleep in."

Since it was barely seven-thirty in the morning, that hardly qualified as sleeping in. Especially after everything they'd been through.

She was wearing jeans and a dark blue sweater that she'd obviously taken from the overnight bag Wyatt had retrieved from her car. No ball cap today. Her hair fell in a shiny tumble on her shoulders. She looked darn good for a woman who clearly hadn't rested as much as she should have. There were still dark circles beneath her eyes that her makeup hadn't hidden.

Declan caught a whiff of that girlie scent she'd had on the day before. "You okay?" he asked.

She nodded. "You?"

He returned the nod, though they both knew the nods were huge lies.

Wyatt's phone buzzed, and he frowned when he looked at the caller ID. "It's a personal call," he said, and he stood and left.

Declan flexed his eyebrows. "Personal," he repeated. He hadn't realized Wyatt was involved with anyone. But then, Wyatt had the rock-star looks of the family, so it wasn't exactly a surprise that he was in a relationship.

"What's going on with the investigation?" She motioned toward the coffeepot, Declan nodded and she poured herself a cup.

"Not much. What's going on with *your* investigation?" Declan waited until her gaze met his before he continued. "I heard you talking on the phone last night."

Actually, he'd heard a lot, since he was listening to make sure she didn't try to sneak out. He hadn't pegged her for reckless, but people did all sorts of crazy things when their lives were on the line.

"I didn't use my cell," Eden said a little defensively. "Just the landline that you said was secure." She paused. "I tried to track down my father."

"How? Because you said you had no idea where he was."

"I don't, but I have the names of the people he's done business with in the past. Plus, the names of a couple of old girlfriends." She shook her head. "All claimed they didn't know his whereabouts."

"You don't believe them?"

She took a big sip of the coffee as if it were the cure for all ills. "Hard to say. One of them might know, but I have to wonder why my father would let someone in on his location when he hadn't told his three daughters."

"Maybe he did tell one. Not you," he quickly added when she shot him a glare. "But one of your sisters."

Eden was shaking her head before he had even finished. "Too risky. They're young and might let something slip. No, if he'd told any of us, it would have been me."

Maybe Zander hadn't wanted to involve any of his girls. Of course, that was something a good father would do, and Declan wasn't about to put that *good* label on any part of Zander's life.

Declan took a notepad and pen and moved it to the empty space at the table that was nearest Eden. "Write down the names of everyone you contacted. I want to press them for info, too."

Her glare morphed to a flat look. "If they wouldn't tell me, they won't tell a marshal."

"I can be charming when I have to be." He let the sarcasm drip off that, but it had an unexpected response.

The corner of Eden's mouth lifted just a fraction. "Yes, you're charming all right."

The smile stayed in place for just a few seconds and then faded. She huffed and dropped down in the chair to start writing on the notepad. "Even if your charm works on these contacts, I don't want my father drawn out just to be killed. And I think we both know that's what this note writer wants to happen."

Oh, yeah. If the person who wrote that note was anyone but Zander, that was exactly what the threat had been designed to do. Draw him out. And not just Zander but Kirby, too.

That wasn't going to happen.

Kirby wasn't strong enough to face down a killer, and even if he were, Declan wouldn't let him. Still, that did lead to some interesting conclusions.

"Whoever wrote the two notes probably knows both Kirby and your father," he pointed out. "And the person wants to use us to get to them. *Us,*" he repeated. "Not your sisters and not my five foster brothers. Because so far, none of the others has been mentioned in any kind of threat."

Eden stopped writing. Met his gaze. "So that's where we start digging. Something that includes me, you, my father and Kirby."

Declan had already been thinking in that direction and had come up with nothing. But there was a long shot that might give them the connection. Or rather might give them Zander. "I want the press to publicize the last note, to bring your father out in the open. Wait," he had to add, because she started to object. "Not so he can be gunned down but so he can help us figure out who's behind the attack."

"And so you can arrest him."

Declan lifted his shoulder. "That, too. He's a fugitive, Eden. If he's alive, I can't just let him walk away."

"I can't let you use me to get to him," she argued.

"Too late." And yeah, this was about to get uglier. "The threat's going out." He checked his watch. "Has gone out," he amended. "The news shows and the papers have probably already picked up on it."

If looks could have maimed, he'd be hurting right about now, because that was how hard her glare was. She was no doubt about to give him a piece of her very angry mind, but Wyatt came back in the room. He glanced at both of them and could probably feel the thick tension between them.

Wyatt shook his head as if disgusted with both of them. "My advice? Stay away from each other."

Obviously, his brother thought this was about the attraction and not the press release. Declan was about to correct him, but Wyatt took his coat from the peg near the back door.

"I've arranged for relief for security detail for Kirby and Stella," Wyatt continued.

Good. He wanted the hospital manned 24/7 until Kirby was home. Then the extra security would be moved to the ranch. "You're not anticipating any trouble at the hospital, are you?" Because something had put that grim look on Wyatt's face.

"No. No problems there. But I need to go into the office and look at some reports." He paused. "Remember the fertility clinic where Ann and I stored our embryos before... Well, before?"

Ann was Wyatt's late wife, and she'd died two and a half years ago. And the *before* referred to when they'd stored the embryos before she'd started her treatment for a rare blood disorder. Treatments that could have left her infertile. Instead, the treatments had failed, and Wyatt had lost his wife.

"There was a theft at the clinic," Wyatt continued. "Several batches of embryos were stolen, including ours."

"Mercy." Eden stood. "Who'd steal embryos?"

Wyatt shrugged, and even though he looked calm on the surface, Declan could tell this was eating away at him. "Some of the embryos were being contested as part of a divorce settlement, and the San Antonio cops think maybe someone was hired to steal them but got ours instead."

So all a mix-up, except this mix-up was massive, since Wyatt had planned on hiring a surrogate so he could finally become the father he'd always wanted to be.

"You need help?" Declan asked.

"No. You've got enough on your plate." He gave them one last glance, and though Wyatt didn't say another word, Declan could hear the repeated warning: *Stay away from each other.* To start, Declan locked up behind Wyatt, and while keeping some distance between them, he looked at the list of names that Eden was writing. She hadn't jotted down her sisters, but he made a mental note to have someone question them about their father. Even if they didn't know anything directly, they might have pieces of info that could lead them to the truth.

"Those are my father's business associates that I called," Eden said, handing him the list. "Well, except for the last one. Janet Klein is an old girlfriend, but she said she hasn't seen him since he was arrested."

Declan knew the woman. He'd interviewed her numerous times after Zander's escape and had even put her under surveillance for a while. And though he believed

Janet was capable of lying—anyone close to Zander could be—he hadn't thought she was hiding her lover.

"All of this could be for nothing." Eden's voice dropped to a raspy whisper. "My father's probably dead anyway."

He was about to remind her that the threat indicated otherwise, but he rethought that. Any part of this could be designed to throw them off track. Like the picture from his childhood. Or the notes themselves. Someone might want them to believe that Zander was part of the danger, but he might be innocent.

Of this anyway.

She stood, brushed past him and went back to the coffeepot to refill her cup. Her hands still weren't too steady. Neither was the rest of her. And it might stay that way until the danger had passed.

"Maybe this is just about you and me," he said. "If someone wanted me dead, then they could have set up this plan to make sure it happened."

Eden sipped her coffee and looked at him from over the rim of her cup. "Same here. If I'd killed you, then I would have ended up in jail. Or killed by the militia group." She paused. "But both of us were supposed to have died in your house. Those gunmen were hired to kill us."

Declan groaned, scrubbed his hand over his face. "Yeah, and that brings us right back to square one."

Well, almost. The investigation was a wash, but now Eden and he were more or less joined at the hip. For him, it was more because he wanted to keep her close in case her father resurfaced.

Or the gunman.

But Declan knew an "or else" look when he saw it, and Eden was no doubt trying to figure out how to ditch him. Maybe because she didn't trust him. Or maybe because if given the chance, he would indeed arrest her father.

Their gazes met. Held. And not just a little holding, either. She finally huffed, "What will it take for you to believe me?"

Declan thought about it a moment. "It's not a matter of belief. It's a matter of whose side you'll choose when and if you figure out your father's behind this."

"If he's behind this, then I'm darn sure not choosing him." She paused for a heartbeat. "But he's not behind this. What if it were your father?" she added before he could answer.

She had a point. He'd never believe that Kirby was guilty of putting him in danger. Or lying about his whereabouts. Lying, period. Kirby wasn't the same sort of man as Zander Gray.

"We need to declare a truce," Eden continued.

That sounded reasonable, and Declan was about to agree when he saw the slight tremble of her bottom lip. Okay, so they were back to that. Her having a normal response to danger. Him having a bad response to her normal one.

Great.

"Truce," he said. But there might be a time limit on it if anything changed in the investigation. Especially if they found anything to implicate her father.

They stood there. Gazes connected again. And with things warm and not so cozy between them. The heat was there all right, but nothing about this felt comfortable. Everything inside him was on alert, and not in a good way, either. For some dumb reason, his body was ignoring the danger warnings and moving right on to the really bad suggestion that he do something even dumber.

Like kiss her.

She didn't back away. Neither did he, and even though he tried to keep the kissing thoughts out of his head, they came anyway. His thoughts were pretty good in that department because he could almost taste her, and it was the prospect of that taste, of the kiss, that had him stepping away just in the nick of time. Of course, his body protested, but that was a mistake he couldn't make.

"The last time I trusted someone I shouldn't have," he said, unbuttoning his shirt, "I got this."

Her eyes widened, and a little burst of air left her mouth. Maybe because she hadn't expected him to bare his chest. But he did that so she could see the scar.

"I slept with a suspect once. Didn't believe she was a suspect until I got between her and her escape vehicle. I learned the hard way that she was not only guilty, she was a decent shot with the .38 she had hidden in her purse."

The look in her eyes changed. No longer truce-like. She reached out as if to touch the scar on his rib cage, but then she jerked back her hand. "Sorry."

He wasn't sure if she was apologizing for the old injury or for the fact she'd almost touched him.

"I've got my own set of baggage," Eden said.

Yeah, he was betting she did.

His phone buzzed. Thank goodness. Well, Declan thought it'd been a good interruption until he saw that the call was from Wyatt. Since his brother had barely had time to get to work, this couldn't be good.

"Eden and you need to get down here right away," Wyatt said the second Declan answered.

Declan put the call on speaker so Eden could hear. "What's going on?"

"You guys are popular today," his brother said. "We

just had not one but two suspects walk in, and both are demanding to talk to the both of you."

"Two?" Declan asked.

"Yeah. And they're already at each other's throats. My advice, get here fast before they try to kill each other. It's Leonard Kane and a guy name Jack Vinson."

Of course, he knew the first one. Leonard was indeed someone Declan wanted to question. But he knew the second name, as well. It wasn't someone he had associated with Zander Gray or the shooting, though.

However, he did have a connection to Kirby.

"Jack Vinson," Eden repeated. "Years ago, he had some business dealings with my father." She shook her head. "But would Jack have anything to do with you or your family?"

Declan tried to keep it short. "Remember the body that was found at the Rocky Creek Children's Facility?"

She nodded. "Jonah Webb, the dead headmaster. Kirby… All of you are suspects as accessory to murder."

"Yeah. And the rangers are also questioning Jack Vinson. He was acquainted with a lot of people connected to Rocky Creek, and he and Webb had had a recent falling-out over the way Webb was running the place."

Last Declan had heard, there was no evidence against the man. So why was he here in Maverick Springs?

"Jack Vinson says he's got information about yesterday's shooting," Wyatt explained. "Says he knows why somebody's trying to kill you."

Chapter Eight

Two suspects. Eden wasn't sure if she should be relieved or suspicious. Either way, this was a strange development, but if it panned out, it could save Declan and her some time. Maybe even their lives.

If the suspects truly cooperated, that is.

Just because they'd arrived voluntarily didn't mean they were at the marshals' office to do anything other than muddy already muddy waters. But then, sometimes people said things they hadn't planned on saying. Maybe that would happen this morning.

"Leonard Kane," Declan repeated, glancing at the two names that he'd jotted down after Wyatt's call. He dropped the notepad with the names on the truck seat next to her, and he drove away from the ranch. Heading into town, where they'd hopefully get the answers they needed.

Yes, Leonard was definitely a suspect since he had a grudge against her father. And against Kirby for killing his son. He'd probably come in because if he hadn't, the marshals would have hauled him in.

But the other suspect was, well, unexpected.

"How much do you know about Jack Vinson?" Declan asked, tapping the second name. He was all lawman now. No trace of the heat that'd stirred between them over coffee in the kitchen. And that was good. They didn't need that interfering with what they had to do.

Eden repeated that to herself.

"As I said, Jack did some business with my father," she explained. "In fact, he was in on that deal that cost Leonard so much money. I can't be sure, but it might have cost Jack money, too." She certainly hadn't known about his connection to Rocky Creek.

"But he wasn't on the list of people you called last night."

She shook her head. "No. I tried, but he wouldn't take my call. But I did speak with him shortly after my father disappeared." She'd contacted anyone and everyone who'd had an association with him. "Like everyone else, Jack said he had no idea where my father was."

Declan made a sound to indicate he was thinking about that. "So why would Jack show up now out of the blue?"

"I don't know." And she didn't. "Your brothers will run a recent background check on him." That was a given. But it might take more than a mere background check to discover why the man had just shown up, claiming to know why someone wanted to kill them. "Do the rangers believe Jack had something to do with Jonah Webb's murder?"

"I'm not sure. They're working with a long list of people they're questioning—including all the former residents and employees of the facility."

Declan was also on that list. Webb's wife had been the one to murder him, but she'd had an accomplice, and that was the person the rangers wanted to identify. So far, they still had a lot of suspects to rule out.

Declan's phone buzzed. "Stella," he said when he

glanced at the screen, and he put the call on speaker. "Is Kirby okay?"

Eden heard the worry in his voice. It was yet another layer of stress when they were already overloaded.

"Kirby's better," Stella answered. "In fact, the doc thinks he'll be able to go home today or tomorrow." She paused. "I asked him about the note. Tried to do it in a roundabout way, but he picked right up on the fact that I was trying to hide something."

Declan flexed his eyebrows, clearly not surprised by that. "Does he have any idea who wrote it?"

Another pause. A long one. "He said it's probably somebody from his past."

"Yeah," Declan agreed, but his eyes said something different. Did he doubt Kirby? "You mentioned the photos to him, especially the one from Germany?"

Even though Eden couldn't see Stella's expression, she could almost feel the hesitation in the woman. What the heck was going on? Was Stella trying to hide something at a time like this?

"Kirby wants to make some calls to ask about those pictures," Stella finally answered.

"No way," Declan snapped. "I don't want him doing anything to put his health at risk."

"Too late. You know how he is when he gets an idea in his hard head. I'm worried, Declan." And the woman's voice cracked. "There are secrets that could come back to haunt him. Haunt all of us," she added.

"What do you mean?" No snapping that time.

"I've said too much. Anything else needs to come from Kirby." And with that, Stella ended the call.

Declan groaned. Then cursed. Eden waited for him to tell her what he intended to do about the news Stella had just dropped on them, but he shot her a glance that let her know the subject was closed.

It wasn't.

Yes, the conversation had had a personal tone to it, but the threat that Declan received was connected to her. *They* were connected. And any secrets that Stella might want to keep couldn't be kept secret.

"You won't talk to Kirby about this," Declan warned her, and he pulled to a stop in the parking lot of the marshals' building.

Since it would have been a lie to agree to that, Eden kept quiet, but she would find a way to speak with Kirby. Or better yet, Stella. The woman obviously knew what was going on, and Eden would make sure she shared it. For now, however, they had a more immediate problem on their hands.

Well, two of them actually.

Declan and she made their way into the building, through the security checkpoint and up the stairs. She didn't even have to step into the sprawling office before she heard a familiar voice.

"You think I'd come here if I was guilty?" Leonard Kane's voice boomed, just short of a full-fledged shout, and Eden soon discovered he was talking to Wyatt, who didn't look at all pleased with their visitor.

The moment Eden appeared in the doorway, Leonard turned toward her and smiled an oily smile that only he and a charlatan could have managed.

She hadn't seen him in nearly three years, but he hadn't changed despite his brain-tumor diagnosis. Iron-gray hair that somehow made him look stronger rather than a man in his mid-fifties. He was wearing starched jeans, a leather jacket, expensive snakeskin boots and a shiny rodeo buckle the size of a grapefruit. Leonard was the opposite of a wallflower and clearly not show-ing any signs of his terminal illness.

"Well, look-y what the cat dragged in," Leonard greeted. Eden wasn't sure if she was the cat or what'd been dragged in. "I was just telling Marshal McCabe here that I'm an innocent man. And a dying one at that. I don't have time for false accusations from the marshals."

"I heard about your brain tumor," Eden said, but didn't offer any sympathy. And wouldn't. Unless she learned he had no part in this.

"Yeah. A kick in the teeth, right?" Leonard said. "The docs can't do a damn thing to cut it out without killing me on the spot. But I guess we all gotta go sometime. My boy, Corey, didn't get much of that time, though."

So they were already on to Kirby killing his son. Eden had figured it wouldn't take him long to bring that up, and maybe Leonard would say enough on the subject that it would give them a solid lead in this investigation.

"I gave the marshal my statement," Leonard went on, "telling him that I was nowhere near your place yester-day and that I ain't holding a grudge against anybody. Especially one of Kirby Granger's boys."

Declan looked past the man and met Wyatt's gaze. "Where's Jack?"

Wyatt hitched his thumb toward the hall. "First inter-rogation room. Best to keep these two apart. Leonard tried to take a swing at him."

"Because Jack's an idiot," Leonard volunteered, his smile turning to a smirk. "Jack's the one who got me in-volved with Zander Gray, and they're the reason I lost a whole boatload of money." The smirk was still in place when his attention came back to Eden. "When you cause a ruckus, you make it a Texas-size one, don't you, girl?"

"I didn't cause a ruckus." She had to get her teeth unclenched so she could finish. "But Marshal O'Malley and I were nearly killed. I'd like to know why."

"And you think I got the answers?" Leonard didn't wait for her to confirm that. "No, Jack's the one claiming to know something. Wish he'd claim to know how to get me back that money he and your daddy cost me. I'm just here to clear my name, give an official statement. And to find out where your daddy is. Because, you see, I figure he's behind all of this and is trying to frame me. I got some old scores to settle, and he's one I'm looking to settle with."

So, it was true. Leonard was cleaning house, but with all the bad he'd done, the world wouldn't miss him.

"Is Zander alive?" Declan asked the man.

Leonard lifted his shoulder. "You should be asking his daughter here, 'cause I don't know. Haven't heard a peep from him. But I'm thinking he's gotta want revenge against you for arresting him."

Declan went closer and got right in Leonard's face. "Why involve Eden?"

"Maybe that wasn't intentional." And though Leonard's voice dripped with sarcasm, Eden had to wonder if there was some truth behind what he'd said. Had her father tried to go after Declan and involved her instead? She didn't want to believe that, but she hadn't seen him in three years. If he was indeed alive, he could be a changed man hell-bent on getting revenge.

"That's it?" Declan's hands went on his hips. "That's all you came here to tell us—that Zander might not have intentionally involved his daughter? Well, that's not enough. Because as far as I'm concerned, you're just as much of a suspect as Zander is."

"Me?" Leonard howled. "I'm innocent. I already said, why would I be here if I was guilty?"

"You would if you didn't want to look guilty. Besides, we had probable cause to haul you in here whether you volunteered or not."

"Well, I didn't have any part in the shooting yesterday out at your place." His cocky look turned to a glare when it landed on the interrogation room where Jack was. "But I'm betting he'll say different. He'll try to pin this on me so it'll get the blame off himself."

Declan glanced at her to see if she knew what Leonard meant, but she had to shake her head. "Why would Jack want to kill Declan and me?" she came out and asked.

Leonard opened his mouth. Closed it. And the smile returned. "You really don't know?"

Declan took a step closer to the man. "Know what?"

His smile got wider. "Oh, you really need to talk to your foster daddy about this."

"I'd rather talk to you about it," Declan argued.

The door to the interrogation room flew open and the man stepped out. Unlike Leonard, Eden had never met Jack Vinson. Also unlike Leonard, he looked like a polished businessman in his navy suit and dark red tie.

"Marshal O'Malley," Jack greeted. "Declan." He said it as if they were old friends. But judging from the way Declan was eyeing him, he'd never met Jack, either.

"Here it comes," Leonard taunted. "He's gonna accuse me of something again. That's the real reason I came down here. This bozo called me and said he was coming in to rat me out. Hard to rat me out, though, when I done nothing wrong."

"Yeah, you're just a model citizen, aren't you?" Wyatt mumbled. Obviously, he'd had his fill of the men before Declan and she had arrived. He looked at his brother.

"Jack claims he has proof of Leonard's involvement in the shooting."

"He ain't got squat," Leonard said at the exact moment that Jack insisted, "I do have proof."

Jack waited until all eyes were on him before he continued. "Word on the street is that a man named Lonnie Reddick was out at Declan's place yesterday, and that he's the hired gun on the run that you've been looking for."

Declan glanced at Harlan, who was behind his desk. "Lonnie Reddick," Harlan repeated. "I'll see what I can find."

"You'll find that Reddick worked for Leonard," Jack supplied. "Still does. Follow the money trail and you'll have proof of the connection."

The profanity that left Leonard's mouth was fast and raw. He moved toward Jack, looking ready to punch him, but Declan stepped between them. "Is that true?" Declan asked Leonard.

"It's true that Reddick worked for me a while back, but I damn sure didn't hire him to kill you yesterday."

Eden stepped closer, as well. "Yes, but did he kill a gunman who could have confirmed who hired all three assassins?"

"No!" Leonard snarled. "I got no reason to hire anyone to come after you."

"No reason except a double motive—to get back at both Kirby and my father," Eden supplied.

Leonard's eyes narrowed to slits, but he aimed his glare at Jack. "You just had to put that in their heads, didn't you? Well, why don't you spill your motive, 'cause I know you got one."

While Leonard was practically spewing venom at the man, Jack remained cool. He eased his hands into his pockets. "It's not a motive. Just the opposite." His gaze returned to Declan. "Stella and I are old friends—"

"Old lovers," Leonard interrupted. "In fact, they were engaged, their wedding just days away when Stella called it off because of Kirby."

"Kirby?" Declan questioned, and judging from his tone, it was the first he was hearing of this. "But Stella and Kirby aren't involved like that."

"Probably because he's too sick to do anything about it." Leonard seemed happy to tell them, too. "But Kirby's always had a hot, dirty thing for Stella. And despite this whole butter-won't-melt-in-Jack's-mouth routine, he'd like nothing more than to get back at Kirby for stealing Stella away from him all those years ago."

"Water under the bridge," Jack said.

Eden looked at both men. Then at Declan to see if he was understanding this. The gunman possibly worked for Leonard. If it was true, that was the connection they'd been looking for.

But she couldn't see how Stella's old flame would play into this.

"There's more," Leonard happily added. "Jack's wife, Beatrice, isn't too happy about the way Kirby and Stella treated her hubby all those years ago. Yeah, Jack wouldn't have married Beatrice if Stella had stayed in his life. But Beatrice is dingbat crazy, so she could mean to get a little revenge of her own. Plus, I figure she's a whole lotta jealous when it comes to Stella, since Jack is still carrying a torch for her."

Jack's jaw muscles stirred a little. "My wife has no part in this." However, he didn't deny his feelings for Stella. He looked at Declan. "Beatrice has spent some time in therapy, but she's fine now."

"She was in a glorified nuthouse." Leonard laughed. "Right where a dingbat belongs."

Eden shook her head. "Okay, I'll bite. Why would Beatrice come after Declan and me because she was upset with Kirby and Stella?"

Leonard made a sound to indicate that the answer was obvious. "Dingbat logic ain't gotta make sense. Some people just carry a grudge for a long time, and when Beatrice married Jack, she married his money. Millions of it. No prenup. And she had to get that money by marrying a hubby who's in love with another woman. She probably figures if she's miserable and locked away in her own loony head, then she should spread that misery around like fertilizer."

"My wife has no part in this," Jack insisted.

Declan obviously didn't believe that. He looked at Harlan. "Do a background check on her."

"Running it now."

Jack mumbled something, shook his head. "I want Beatrice left out of this investigation. Stella, too. Whatever's going on here has nothing to do with them."

"Don't be so sure about that," Leonard continued. He was smiling again when he looked at Declan, and that smile put a knot in her stomach. "Good ol' Jack here helped Stella rig the paperwork that got you out of that Rocky Creek hellhole."

Declan's attention slashed to Jack, and the man didn't deny it. "You mean the paperwork that put me in Kirby's foster care?"

Some of Jack's cool exterior evaporated. "Yes. I admit it. I helped with the paperwork. That part's true. But what Leonard's going to claim is that I also helped murder Jonah Webb. I didn't."

Eden wasn't sure she believed him. Or that this mattered, but judging from the glance that Wyatt and Declan exchanged, maybe it did.

"Yeah, you're getting it now," Leonard said, obviously noticing that glance, too. "Jack's in the hot seat, maybe on the verge of being charged as an accessory to Webb's murder. No statute of limitations on that. His butt could land in jail for life. Or worse. So how far do you think Jack or his dingbat wife would go to stop Kirby from ratting him out?"

"Not *that far,*" Jack insisted.

"Are you saying that Jack or Beatrice would try to kill Declan and me?" Eden pressed Leonard. "How would that keep him out of jail?"

"He's not trying to kill you. What happened yesterday was a message to Kirby. Bite the bullet and confess to the Webb murder, or there'll be hell to pay—with his all-grown-up foster kid."

Jack stared at the man who'd just accused him of attempted murder. "That's ridiculous. From what I heard, Declan and Eden were in grave danger. They could have been killed."

"We could have been," Eden verified.

But no one seemed to hear her.

"That's what Lonnie Reddick was all about," Leonard said. "The man hasn't worked for me for months, but Jack or his wife knew he could hire him to take out the gunmen firing those shots at you two. He knew Kirby would understand what was going on."

That created another shouting match between the two men, but Eden dropped back a step so she could take it all in.

Had Jack really set this up?

"If he did it, it's a stupid way to send a message," Declan said, as if reading her mind. "My brothers would have gone after him if I'd been killed. And if you'd been killed, *I* would have gone after him."

She tried not to be flattered about that last part. Especially since in that particular scenario she'd be dead. But she was grateful that Declan would find the culprit if something did indeed happen to her.

And that probably didn't have anything to do with the heat between them.

No. He was first and foremost a lawman.

"This meeting is over," Jack announced. For a moment Eden thought he was going to storm out, but he stopped right in front of Declan.

"If I find out you're behind this, I'm arresting you," Declan warned him.

"If I were behind this, I'd let you arrest me," Jack countered. There was no ripe anger in his voice, only the glare that he aimed at Leonard. "My advice? Don't believe a word he says and find an excuse—any excuse—to put him behind bars."

"I'll be looking to do the same to you," Declan assured him.

Jack stared at Declan a moment later, added something under his breath that Eden didn't catch and walked out.

"You should be arresting him," Leonard grumbled.

"No evidence. *Yet.* But I will be looking for some. Looking for something on you, too," Declan told Leonard.

Leonard glanced around, maybe trying to decide where to go with this. Obviously he hadn't gotten what he wanted. Jack hadn't been arrested. He looked down at his hands, and Eden saw that he was shaking.

"Damn tumor," Leonard grumbled. He shoved his hands in his pockets. "They say it'll get worse. The headaches, too. And then I'll just keel over." He stared at Eden. "Let's hope I can get my goodbyes finished before that happens."

"Is that some kind of threat?" she asked. And she didn't back down from him.

"The only people who should feel threatened are the ones with a reason to be. You got a reason to be threatened by me, Eden?"

Declan didn't give her a chance to answer. He stepped between them. "Can you finish interviewing him?" Declan asked Wyatt. "I need to talk to Kirby."

No doubt to ask him about Stella's cryptic comments. But Kirby would have to be questioned about this, too. All of the danger was starting to lead right back to him and maybe what had happened at Rocky Creek all those years ago.

Judging from Leonard's renewed scowl, he didn't appreciate being handed off to Wyatt or putting an end to his little word games, but Eden hoped that Declan's brother could get some usable information from the man.

"I'd like to go with you when you question Kirby," she said to Declan once Leonard was out of earshot.

"I'm not *questioning* him. He's too weak for that. I only want to talk to him for a few moments."

Eden didn't even try to stop herself from groaning. "You can't let your personal feelings play into this. Besides, I'm sure Kirby wants you to be safe, and if he knows anything that can make that happen, then he'll tell you."

She hoped.

Though Kirby might not be willing to share that information with her.

Declan's mouth tightened, but he didn't argue. "Let's go," he snarled.

"Someone's on the phone for you," Harlan called out before they could leave.

Declan and she turned back around, but it took her a moment to realize that Harlan was talking to her, not Declan.

Harlan had his hand over the receiver of the landline phone so that the caller wouldn't be able to hear. "He says it's important," he added.

Eden shook her head. No one would know to be calling her here at the marshals' office. Unless it was the bodyguard she'd hired to watch her sisters, and if he couldn't have reached her with just a call, then he might have contacted law enforcement.

Oh, God.

Maybe something bad had happened to them.

She hurried across the room and nearly ripped the phone from Harlan's hand. "Is everything all right?" And she couldn't ask it fast enough.

"No. Far from it."

Eden's stomach went to her knees. Not the bodyguard. But it was a voice she recognized.

Her father's.

He was alive.

The relief flooded through her. Quickly followed by the concern and the realization that she had both Harlan and Declan staring at her and waiting.

"Don't say anything," her father warned her. "And find out a way to ditch Marshal O'Malley. Because I need to see you *now*. And I need to see you alone."

Chapter Nine

Eden didn't say a word, and Declan couldn't hear what the caller was telling her. Whatever it was, it couldn't be good, and they already had enough bad news to deal with.

"I understand," she finally said and pressed the button to end the call. Eden eased the phone back onto Harlan's desk. She didn't look at him but instead kept her attention on the phone.

"What happened?" Declan asked, and he glanced at Harlan, who just shook his head.

"The caller was using a burner," Harlan let him know after he checked the laptop next to the phone.

No way to trace it, which meant this call might have been from the gunman. Whoever it was and whatever he'd said, it had caused the color to drain from Eden's face. She didn't say anything, and that told him loads about the call. If it'd been a threat or warning about immediate danger to her sisters, she would have blurted it out so they could spring into action.

Finally, her gaze came to his, and she took him by the arm. "We have to talk." With the others watching, she led Declan out into the hall. "Please don't make me regret telling you this." Her voice was a shaky whisper.

And Declan knew who'd just called. "Where's your father?"

"He didn't say." She swallowed hard.

"But he wants to meet with you."

She nodded. "*Alone.* He said he's not guilty, that he was framed for trying to kill the witness who was going to testify against him."

Of course, Zander would say that. It was rare for a criminal to admit guilt, but he wasn't likely to convince Eden of the possibility that her father could be a dangerous man. "Where's the meeting?"

Eden turned away from him. She would have avoided his gaze completely if Declan hadn't caught her chin and forced eye contact. "Where and when?" he demanded.

Still, she took her time answering, and it seemed as if she changed her mind several times about telling him this. "Half hour. A pond about ten miles out of town. It's on West Farm Road."

Declan knew the exact spot. It was a remote location with almost no traffic. Plenty of trees for cover. Plenty of places to hide a vehicle, too. Unfortunately, it also had escape routes, since there were several ranch trails that rimmed the pond.

"I own that land," Declan explained. And he doubted that was a coincidence. Zander had likely chosen it because he knew it would dig at Declan. Had Zander also known that Eden would tell him about the meeting location?

And he went a little further with that thought.

Was Eden telling him the whole truth?

She wouldn't lead him into a trap. But he rethought that and groaned. Apparently, this attraction had made him a complete idiot, because he shouldn't trust her.

But he did.

After everything they'd been through, he didn't think she'd put him in the path of more bullets. And he hoped like the devil that was true.

"I need you to stay here," Declan told her.

She didn't just shake her head. Eden took him by the shoulders. "If I'm not at the meeting, my father won't be, either."

"That's a chance I'll have to take."

"And it's a dumb chance." She huffed, and it seemed to take her a moment to rein in her temper. "If I don't step out near that pond, then my father will just disappear into the woods. I don't want that. I want to know the information he has about all of this."

Yeah, so did Declan, but he wasn't sure it was worth the risk.

"And I need to make sure he's okay. I'm going to that meeting," Eden insisted. "And if you leave me behind, I'll just figure out another way to get there. My being there is the best way to keep you safe."

Now he groaned. "It's not your job to keep me safe."

Her eyes narrowed a little. "I can say the same thing right back to you. I didn't ask for your protection." And then her eyes narrowed a lot. "I'm not backing down on this."

Nope. She wouldn't. Any fool could see the determination in her eyes, which weren't so darn bedroom at the moment. She'd find a way there all right, and nothing short of putting her in a jail cell would make her stay put. Declan considered doing just that—locking her up—but there was something else playing into this.

Without Eden, he wouldn't be able to get close to her father.

Zander had known exactly where she was. It meant he was watching them or had hired someone to do that.

And depending on how long he'd been watching them, Zander might indeed have information about the attack. Maybe even firsthand information that he'd volunteer or let slip when Declan talked to him.

Hoping he didn't regret this, he leaned back inside the squad room, caught Harlan's attention and motioned for him to join them.

"This meeting has to stay a secret," Eden insisted when she realized what was going on.

"Not a chance. We're not going out there without some kind of backup."

"I'm your backup," she protested.

But he ignored her and turned to Harlan. "I need you to follow us out to Old Saunder's pond. And if Zander Gray calls back, leave instructions to give him my cell number."

Harlan mumbled some profanity. "You're meeting with Eden's father?"

"Yeah. Right after I call the hospital."

Harlan didn't ask why he was doing that. His brother knew. Declan needed to ask Kirby about the things Leonard and Jack had said. It was probably nothing. He hoped. But it wouldn't feel like nothing until Kirby reassured him that he'd had no part in this.

Webb's murder was a different matter.

Even though there'd been no proof, before now anyway, as to who'd helped Sarah Webb murder her husband, Declan had always known that her accomplice could be a member of his foster family. Now he had another suspect to add to that list of possible accomplices.

Jack Vinson.

He had to figure out if Jack was trying to pressure Kirby into confessing to a crime he didn't commit. Or if Beatrice Vinson was so jealous of Stella that she was behind all of this.

Still mumbling, Harlan went back inside the squad room.

"I want my gun while we're at this meeting," Eden said.

Only then did he remember the sheriff had taken it from her since she'd fired it at the assassins who'd tried to kill them. It would have to be processed as part of the crime scene.

"My backup weapon's in the glove compartment. Come on." Declan grabbed their coats and they headed downstairs and to his truck. "But there are rules about this meeting. My rules. You'll follow them, or we'll drive right back to town and you won't see your father."

Her gaze slid to his. "What rules?"

"Easy ones." He hoped. "You stay behind me, and if anything goes wrong, you get on the ground. Agree to them or stay here. That's the only choice I'm giving you." He wasn't budging on this, either.

"Agreed," she finally said. "But if my father sees you with me, he won't show his face," Eden warned him right back.

Maybe. "I'm not letting you meet him alone. He could be behind these attempts to kill us."

"He won't hurt me."

Yeah, Declan was counting heavily on that. But he was also counting on backup in case his instincts were dead wrong.

Eden continued to argue, but the moment he unlocked the truck and she got inside, she took his gun from the glove compartment. Extra ammo, too, which she crammed into her pockets.

"Repeating myself here, but it's a bad idea for you to come with me," she grumbled.

"A lot of things happening between us fall into the bad-idea category." And with that obvious statement out of the way, he turned his attention to their surroundings.

Declan glanced around to see if they were being watched, then he eased out of the parking lot, making sure no one followed them. He didn't want to drive too fast because there might be ice on the roads, and he wanted to give Harlan a chance to catch up with them. Besides, he needed a little time to speak to Stella.

Declan tried her number and was a little surprised when she answered on the first ring—as if she'd been expecting him. He didn't want to put the call on speaker, though Eden no doubt wanted to hear every word. But this conversation was something he might need to keep in the family.

For now anyway.

Of course, Eden was trying to do the same with this meeting with her father. Still, a phone call wasn't dangerous. Well, not in a bullet-flying sort of way like a face-to-face encounter with Zander might be. But he could learn something from this call that Declan wasn't sure he wanted to learn.

"I just got off the phone with Jack Vinson," Stella immediately told him. "He said you had a meeting with Leonard Kane."

"We did." And Declan left it at that. If Jack and she had talked, then Stella already knew what he wanted from her.

Answers.

Or better yet, a denial of Kirby's involvement. But Stella didn't volunteer anything.

Eden mumbled something he didn't catch, but she was

clearly frustrated that she couldn't hear what Stella was saying, and she scooted across the seat closer to him. As far as her seat belt would allow, and until they were arm to arm. Not the best position, especially when she put her face next to his.

"Is Kirby up to seeing us?" Declan asked when Stella's silence continued.

"He's feeling better. And I'd like to keep it that way for a while longer." She paused, and even though he didn't hear her sniffling or anything, Declan could sense that this was not a conversation she wanted to have. "Maybe this can keep for a day or two."

"In a day or two, Eden and I could be dead." He hated just to toss that out there, but it was the truth. If the danger had been directed only at him, Declan would have gladly backed off for as long as Stella deemed necessary, but this had to stop.

"Look, I don't want to make Kirby any worse," Declan continued, "but you and I both know if he could do anything to prevent another attack, then he'd do it."

"Yes, he would." Another pause.

"You know you're going to have to tell me the truth?" Declan asked her.

"I know. But I'm not sure if the truth will help."

Declan didn't like the sound of that. He'd wanted Stella to deny there were any secrets. Especially secrets that had anything to do with Kirby's involvement not just in this situation but in Webb's murder.

"I need to hear it," Declan insisted.

The seconds crawled by. "Tonight then."

Declan had plenty to do between now and then. That included this little chat with Zander. But he suddenly wanted nothing more than to hurry to the hospital and demand the answers that Stella didn't want him to know.

Stella ended the call, and Declan put away his phone.

Eden backed away a little, but her stare stayed on him. "If Kirby knows anything about—"

"Then he'll tell me," Declan interrupted.

"Us," she corrected.

Declan wanted to insist that particular conversation be private, but this wasn't a privacy situation. There was indeed an *us* in this, and it wasn't based solely on the attraction. Eden's life was on the line, too.

"After we're finished with Zander, we'll deal with Kirby," he assured her, though he wasn't sure how to go about doing that.

"Finished," she repeated under her breath. "You do know that my father isn't just going to let you arrest him. And I don't want another shoot-out."

Neither did he, and that was why he had to take some basic precautions. He slowed to a crawl until he spotted Harlan's dark blue truck coming up behind them, and Declan turned onto one of the ranch trails.

He looked at the dirt and gravel surface to see if anyone had driven on it recently, but it was hard to tell since it was scabbed with ice.

Eden glanced around. "Where exactly are we going?"

"This trail takes us to the backside of the pond."

Of course, her father could have had someone hidden in the trees, watching them. He might know their every move, but this was just a basic precaution. Besides, the trees gave them much better cover than being out on the farm road itself.

Harlan stayed behind him, both vehicles bobbing across the uneven surface. Declan kept watch. So did Eden. Her gaze fired all around, and she had a death grip on the gun she was holding.

Declan followed the trail, moving deeper into the

trees. It was darker here since the tall live oaks choked out what little sun there was. They also choked the trail since some were so close that the branches scraped against the sides of his truck. Again, there were no signs that anyone had been here. At least not with a vehicle.

"The pond's just over there." Declan pointed to his right, but the water wasn't in sight yet. "We'll park and walk the rest of the way."

At least once they were outside he'd be able to hear footsteps or some other indication that they weren't alone in these woods. Of course, it'd be next to impossible to hear a shooter who was already in place.

Declan turned, intending to move off the trail and into a narrow clearing, but he spotted a pile of leaves just ahead. It didn't look like anything Mother Nature had formed, so he hit his brakes.

But it was too late.

The truck jolted. Eden and he did, too, and if they hadn't been wearing their seat belts, they would have slammed into the dash and steering wheel. Thankfully, Harlan was able to stop in time and didn't plow right into them.

Eden gasped, lifted her gun. "What happened?"

"I'm pretty sure someone put spikes or nails on the trail." Because whatever he'd hit had taken out both front tires. It'd also left them sitting ducks.

Hell. This was not the way he'd wanted things to play out.

Declan drew his gun. Looked around. Harlan's truck hadn't been disabled, so they'd need to use it to get the heck out of there.

"Move fast," Declan told Eden, and he opened his truck door. "Stay right with me." They started walking with her pressed against the truck and with him in front of her.

"See anyone?" Harlan asked, stepping from his truck, as well.

"No." But Declan had no sooner said it than he did see *something*. Movement behind one of the larger oaks. Whoever was there ducked back out of sight, and that couldn't be a good sign.

"Step away from the truck," someone shouted. "And keep your hands in the air so I can see them."

Declan saw the gun then. And not just one, but several, all pointed right at them.

The three of them were surrounded.

Chapter Ten

Eden didn't have time to react. But Declan sure did. He hooked his arm around her and dragged her to the ground.

Her heart slammed against her chest, and she braced herself for the gunshots. However, no shots came. Just the eerie silence and the sound of her own heartbeat crashing in her ears.

"Stand up," someone said. It was her father. "And remember that part about keeping your hands where I can see them."

Eden tried to get up, but Declan shoved her right back to the ground. He certainly didn't do as her father had ordered. He took aim at one of the shadowy figures behind a tree. Harlan pointed his gun at another one. Eden didn't do any pointing because one of those shadows was her father.

"O'Malley, if I wanted you dead, you already would be," her father said.

"Is that supposed to make me trust you?" Declan snapped.

"No, but this might."

She lifted her head just a fraction and saw her father step out from behind one of the trees. He was armed, a gun in his right hand and a large manila envelope in his left. He was dressed like a soldier going to combat, with camo and gear, and he had a black baseball cap slung low over his face.

The relief flooded through her—he was alive—but the relief was soon followed by the fear that he might not stay that way for long. This could easily turn into a gunfight if she didn't do something to defuse it.

"Declan saved my life," she volunteered, and despite the fact that he was trying to keep her on the ground, Eden managed to wiggle away from him and get to her feet. However, Declan did stop her from going closer to her father. "I don't want him or his brother hurt."

Declan cursed. Stood up. And stepped in front of her after he shot her a glare. "There are rules, and you just broke them."

"Admirable," her father said before she could respond to Declan. "You're trying to protect my daughter. Ironic, huh? Since you'd like nothing better than to see me dead."

"Not ironic. Your daughter didn't try to kill a witness and then escape from jail."

Her father shook his head. "I didn't try to kill a witness, either." He walked toward them and met her gaze. "I would give you a hug, but the marshal here wouldn't like that."

"I'm not sure I would, either," she answered. It hurt to say that, and it hurt to see the flash of surprise go through her father's eyes. "You should have let us know you were alive."

"Couldn't risk you telling the cops. Or the marshals. You always were a do-gooder, Eden."

His voice wasn't exactly cold, but the look he gave her was. There'd never been a lot of affection between them. Her father wasn't, well, fatherly. But she loved him as only a daughter could.

"I wouldn't have turned you in." She had to clear her throat and repeat it so that it was more than a whisper. "I would have tried to help you."

The corner of her father's mouth lifted. "And now you're sleeping with the enemy."

She was sure she blinked and then quickly shook her head.

"Eden's in my protective custody," Declan growled.

"And she spent the night with you," her father growled back.

"Not *with* me." Declan's jaw tightened. "Under the same roof, and she did that because she's in serious danger. Someone wants me and your daughter dead. I'm thinking that someone might be you."

Eden pulled in her breath and waited. Prayed, too. Her father couldn't be involved in this.

"Not me," her father insisted. "I wouldn't do anything to hurt Eden or any of my girls. The only reason I've stayed away is because it's safer for them."

"Safer for you, too," Declan reminded him. "After all, you're not in jail."

"Yes, but that doesn't mean there aren't people who want to silence me." Zander made a nervous glance around the woods. "More than once someone's tried to kill me, and damn if I know why. And before you ask, I don't know who's trying to kill you, either. Could be Leonard or Jack. Or Jack's crazy wife. Maybe Kirby."

"Not Kirby," Harlan and Declan said in unison.

"Someone from your past then," her father continued. "Maybe the same person who killed your family in Germany."

Because Declan's arm was touching hers, she felt

every muscle go stiff. That was probably the one connection he didn't want mentioned here. Because he had no leads, and the case had been cold for decades. Still, there'd been that photo included with the more recent ones, so this might indeed all be threaded together.

Her father took a step closer and dropped the thick envelope at Declan's feet. "There's the proof that I'm innocent."

Declan didn't reach down to retrieve the envelope. He kept his attention staked to her father. Beside him, Harlan was trying to keep an eye on the gunman. From what she could tell, there were two of them, at least, but they were both staying behind cover.

"What kind of so-called evidence do you claim to have?" Declan asked.

"The kind that I want you to investigate so I can clear my name. I can hire muscle, but I can't do this investigation on my own."

"I'm not interested in clearing your name. I have bigger fish to fry right now."

"Right." Not said sarcastically, but her father seemed to be in agreement. "I have something that might help speed things along."

He motioned toward one of the men lurking behind the tree, and someone stepped out. Not a gunman. This person was handcuffed, and he staggered forward when the gunman gave him a shove.

Eden didn't recognize the handcuffed man, but judging from Harlan's and Declan's reactions, they did.

"Lonnie Reddick," Declan mumbled.

The missing gunman. And possibly the same man who'd tried to murder them at Declan's house the day before. At a minimum, he'd murdered his wounded comrade before he could tell them who'd hired them to launch the attack.

"I figured you'd like the chance to talk to Reddick," her father went on, "and in turn, I want you to look into the papers in that envelope."

"I'll look at them, but I'm not making any promises," Declan insisted.

Her father gave a slight huff. "Find out who set me up. And keep my daughter safe. I'd do it myself, but I'm not exactly in the position for it." His gaze came to Eden. "I have to go, but as soon as I can, I'll come back to see you."

She nodded and felt the tears burn her eyes. Her father couldn't stay, she knew that, but Eden also knew that even if Declan proved his innocence, he'd still be arrested for breaking out of jail and becoming a fugitive. She doubted he'd just voluntarily go back to prison, and that meant he could still be killed while trying to evade the law.

And in this case, the law was Declan.

With his gun still aimed and ready, Harlan went forward, latched on to Reddick and hauled him toward his truck. "What should we do about him?" Harlan asked, tipping his head to her father.

Declan met her father's gaze head-on. "I can't just let you leave."

"And I can't let you arrest me," her father argued.

Her heart nearly stopped, because they were not the sort of men who backed down. She couldn't lose her father now that she'd just learned he was alive. But she couldn't lose Declan, either.

Eden silently cursed both of them. And the stalemate that followed. They stood there, the bitter cold wind whipping at them. Guns aimed.

"Please," Eden whispered. But she wasn't sure which one of them she wanted to give in.

"Boss?" one of the gunmen yelled.

But that was the only warning they got before the sound cracked though the air.

Someone had fired a shot.

DECLAN COULDN'T MOVE fast enough.

He threw himself against Eden and pulled her to the side of his truck and then onto the ground. Beside him, Harlan did the same with Reddick, and all of them cursed the bullets that started to slam around them. Harlan wedged both Reddick and himself in between the two trucks.

Zander cursed, too, and he dropped down just a few feet away from them. For just that split second of time, Declan had thought the shots might be coming from Zander's own hired guns, but judging from the man's fierce reaction, someone else was shooting.

Just what they didn't need.

Of course, this could be some kind of ploy set up by Zander to make it easier for him to escape, but if so, it was stupid. Because any one of those bullets could ricochet off something and hit Eden or the rest of them.

"He's to your right!" one of Zander's men behind the tree shouted.

Declan's attention was already aimed in that direction because it was where the shots were coming from. There was a cluster of trees, so thick that it would make a good hiding place. Of course, the question was how had this guy managed to sneak up on Zander's men? Or had he already been in place before Eden and he had even arrived?

"Stop the SOB!" Zander shouted.

A shot slapped into the ground right next to Eden and sent up a spray of dirt and pebbles. They had to move. But there weren't exactly a lot of options. Getting back into the truck would be a huge risk. Plus, Harlan was parked behind him, and going forward would mean moving closer to the shooter. With the front tires already out, that didn't seem like a good option. Of course, none of their options seemed good at this point.

"Can you see him?" Eden asked. Her breath was racing and every muscle in her body was tense.

Declan shook his head and tried to keep watch. And there was a lot to watch. Eden's father for one. Even though Zander was flat on the ground, he was still armed, and he could turn that weapon on Declan so he could try to escape.

To his left, he heard Harlan talking, and he realized he was calling for backup. Good. Maybe it'd arrive in time, but he cursed himself and their situation. Because once again, Eden was in danger.

Finally, Declan saw some movement in the tree cluster. So did Zander's men, because shots started to go in that direction. They were returning fire, and it might be enough to get the guy to stop. Declan figured there was a slim-to-none chance of keeping him alive so he could question him, but at least they had Reddick.

If they could keep him alive, that is.

He also had to consider that this attack was meant to kill Reddick, since he could likely spill a lot of details that a would-be killer would want to keep hidden. So there could be multiple targets here. Zander, Reddick, Eden or himself.

Or maybe all of them.

The more he learned about this investigation, the more he realized that everything was tangled together.

And they had to dodge these bullets if they ever hoped to untangle it.

More shots came. Seemingly from every direction. God knows how many people were actually shooting out there. In fact, their attacker could have plenty of backup of his own.

"Get Eden out of here now!" her father shouted, and Declan was pretty sure Zander was talking to him. "We'll settle our score later."

The shots continued, making it hard to think or hear, but Declan had to come up with some kind of plan, because this guy wasn't stopping. There had to be at least two of them, since the shots were coming nonstop.

"Crawl beneath my truck," Declan told her. So far, there'd been no shots fired there, but that didn't mean there wasn't another shooter out in the woods. One with a better shot at the other side of his truck.

Eden didn't move, and he could practically feel the hesitation in every part of her body. "I need that envelope," she said, and that was the only warning she gave Declan before she snaked out, grabbed it and then got back behind him.

Later, he'd chew her out for that, but for now, he just wanted to get her the heck out of there.

"Move under my truck," Declan ordered.

Thankfully, Eden didn't argue this time. She got on her belly and started crawling. Declan kept an eye on Zander, and he considered motioning for Harlan to get moving, too. But there was a problem. An escape would be next to impossible with a prisoner, and Declan had to consider that the complication was all part of Zander's plan.

Whatever plan that was.

If they all piled into Harlan's truck, Zander could escape, and Harlan, Eden and he could be left with Red-dick, who might try to fight his way out of the small space. With the gunmen firing shots, things could turn deadly fast. Still, it was riskier to stay put.

"Don't leave cover," Declan told Eden when she had reached the far side underneath his truck. He motioned for Harlan to get moving, as well. Not toward the shoot-ers, but toward what he hoped was the safe side of their vehicles.

"I'll be in touch," Declan warned Zander.

"Just read the papers in that envelope," Zander in-sisted.

He would. Once they were safely out of this, and he refused to believe that wouldn't happen. Declan scram-bled under the truck with Eden.

"What about my father?" she asked. She was breath-ing through her mouth now, the air gusting in and out, and she looked as terrified as she sounded.

"He wants you out of here," he reminded her. And, yeah, that wasn't the answer Eden wanted to hear, but Declan wanted her out of there, too.

In the distance he heard a welcome sound. Sirens. Probably one or more of his brothers responding. They wouldn't come in with guns blazing and bullets flying, but at least they were nearby in case things went from bad to worse.

Declan moved ahead of Eden so that he could look out. No sign of any shooters. Just Harlan, who had a meaty grip on Reddick's shirt collar. He and his brother made eye contact, and Declan motioned for Harlan to get in through the passenger's side.

The seconds slowed to a crawl, but Harlan finally stuffed both himself and Reddick into the truck. However, Reddick had barely managed to get in when there was another shot.

This one sent Declan's heart to his knees.

Because it hadn't been fired from the tree cluster. No. This one had slammed into the front of Harlan's truck.

Damn.

Either the shooter had moved or this was his backup. And it wasn't just one shot. They came crashing through his brother's truck.

Declan took aim, trying to pinpoint the shooter's location, and he fired. Judging from the sound of it, he hit a tree, but it must have been close enough because the shooter paused. It was just enough time for Harlan to dive onto the seat and get behind the wheel.

The shooter fired again. And this time, the bullet didn't go into a tree. Declan knew that sound. Bullet into flesh. Reddick snapped forward, his body twisting into an unnatural angle, before falling to the ground.

Someone had shot Reddick in the back of the head.

Declan didn't have to touch the man to know he was dead. It'd been a very accurate kill shot, and just like that, no more bullets came at them. Well, not from this angle anyway. The shots continued on the other side of the trucks.

"Get her out of here!" Zander yelled again.

Declan wanted nothing more, but he had to wait. And he didn't like what he heard. No more shots, but someone was running. The assassin, no doubt. Just as Reddick had done at his house, the gunman had been killed. And so had any link to the person who'd hired him.

"Let's move now," Declan insisted.

He gripped Eden's arm and they scurried out from beneath the truck. It was a short trek, but not an easy one, since they had to climb over Reddick's body. The moment they were inside, Harlan threw his truck into Reverse and gunned the engine.

Declan held his breath. Said a prayer, too, and that prayer was apparently answered because no other bullets came their way. The gunmen, however, continued to shoot, and the bullets pelted the ground near Declan's truck.

"Oh, God," Eden said on a gasp.

That snagged his attention, and Declan followed her gaze to her father. Zander was no longer on the ground but had gotten up to a crouching position. He aimed his gun in the direction of the trees where the shots were coming.

Declan couldn't tell if Zander managed to pull the trigger, but he saw the man's body jerk back. No doubt from a bullet slamming into his chest.

Eden screamed, the sound echoing over the bullet blasts and the roar of the engine. She would have bolted from the truck if Declan hadn't held on to her.

"My father's been shot," she said, and she kept repeating it.

Declan caught her face and forced her to look him in the eyes. "Stay in the truck with Harlan. He'll get you to safety."

Declan hoped.

"Slow down just for a second," he told Harlan.

Harlan cursed, called him a bad name mixed with some profanity, but he slowed just enough for Declan to jump from the truck. He hit the ground running.

Directly toward the shooters.

Chapter Eleven

Eden threw the envelope on the floor and tried to pull Declan back into the truck, but she wasn't fast enough. He ducked behind a tree, leaned out and fired. She couldn't see where his shot landed because Harlan kept going, the truck flying in Reverse.

"We have to help Declan," she insisted. "And my father."

Harlan didn't respond. He kept his eyes on the side mirror and maneuvered around a curve. Once he was on the other side, he stopped. Without the noise from the engine and the dirt and rocks slapping against the undercarriage, Eden could hear something surprising.

Silence.

However, she did hear something else. Sirens. They were getting closer, and it didn't take long before the blue lights were flashing all around them. The cruiser came to a stop behind them, and both Wyatt and the local sheriff, Rico Geary, cracked open their doors. Harlan did the same.

"Declan's out there," Harlan relayed to them. "Zander Gray, too, and at least three gunmen. There's also a dead body, Lonnie Reddick."

That brought Wyatt out of the cruiser, and with his gun drawn he walked toward them. "You two okay?"

Harlan looked at her. Nodded. "Don't know about Zander or Declan, though."

"My father was shot," Eden volunteered.

Wyatt spared them both a glance, but continued up the trail, using the trees and shrubs for cover. Sheriff Geary did the same on the other side, but when he reached the truck, Harlan got out.

"I need you to stay with Eden," he told the sheriff.

Geary didn't argue, but Harlan had only made it a few steps when she heard someone shout. "It's me. Don't shoot."

Declan.

Despite the sheriff's attempts to stop her, Eden bolted from the truck and started running. The relief was instant. So was the fear of how close he'd come to dying. Again.

She didn't think. Eden ran right to Declan and was surprised when he pulled her into his arms. He brushed a kiss on her cheek. Pulled back, examined her face. She did the same to him. No injuries, thank goodness. And she didn't kiss his cheek. She pressed her lips to his for several moments.

"What about my father?" she asked, hating to hear the answer.

Declan only shook his head. "He wasn't there when I got back. His men must have gotten him out. But I think he was wearing Kevlar because I didn't see any blood."

She replayed all those horrible images and realized he was right. Her father had fallen to the ground, clutching his chest, but there'd been no blood.

"You went back for my father," she said under her breath. Their eyes met, and whether he would admit it or not, he hadn't done that just so he could arrest him. Declan had done that for her. "Thank you."

"I didn't do it for him," Declan quickly let her know.

"We need to get out of here," Harlan reminded them before they could say anything else. "Those gunmen could come back."

"Yes," the sheriff agreed, "and I need to get the rangers out here to help with this crime scene." He looked at Declan. "Unless you want to do that yourself."

Declan shook his head, looped his arm around her waist and got them moving toward Harlan's truck. The sheriff had to move the cruiser, but Harlan was finally able to get turned around so they could drive out of there.

Eden glanced behind them one last time, both hoping to get a glimpse of her father and hoping she didn't. Because if any of the lawmen saw him, they'd arrest him. But at least she would know for certain that he was alive and unharmed.

"Either of you need to see a doctor?" Harlan asked. They both shook their heads. "Then I'm headed to the office. We've got a hell of a big mess to sort through."

They couldn't argue with that. Heaven knows how long it'd take to go through a crime scene that large.

Declan picked up the envelope that she'd tossed on the floor, but he didn't open it right away. He kept watch. So did Harlan.

No doubt in case there was another attack.

Her body was braced for one. Every nerve seemed to be right near the surface. And worse, this latest attack hadn't ended anything. They now had a dead gunman who couldn't give them any information. And her father was on the run again.

"You need to level your breathing," Declan told her.

Only then did she realize she wasn't just breathing fast, she was on the edge of hyperventilating. He slipped his arm around her, eased her to him, and Eden dropped her head on his shoulder.

It was wrong to take comfort from him this way, and Harlan obviously didn't approve of it, judging from the grunt he made. But Eden didn't pull away. She was afraid if she did, she might fall apart.

However, Declan didn't fall apart. With her still cradled against his arm, he opened the envelope and took out a handful of papers.

"They're bank records," Declan said, riffling through the pages. "Leonard Kane's."

That instantly got her attention, since Leonard was one of their suspects. "Do they show a huge payment at the time someone attempted to murder the witness?" Because it was that attempt that had ultimately sent her father to jail.

"There are a lot of big payments here." Declan continued to thumb through them but then stopped. "I'm betting your father didn't obtain these with Leonard's permission."

Even with the adrenaline still spiking through her, it didn't take Eden long to see where he was going with this. "So you wouldn't be able to use any of this to charge Leonard with a crime."

"Or even to get a court order," Harlan added. "Still, we'll give them to my brother, Clayton, and see what he can do with them."

Mercy. She didn't want Leonard or anyone else who was guilty to go free, but maybe the papers would still clear her father. Not officially. But in Declan's mind anyway. If that happened, he might dig harder to get to the truth about what had really happened.

Harlan pulled into the parking lot of the marshals' building, and as before, Declan rushed her inside. Unlike before, the office was practically deserted. Probably because the others had responded to the scene or were guarding Kirby and Stella. The only person in the room was one of Declan's brothers, Clayton.

"Any news about my father?" she immediately asked.

But Clayton shook his head and looked at Declan. "We do have a visitor though. Beatrice Vinson. I didn't call her in," he added. "She just showed up here about ten minutes ago and demanded to talk to Eden and you."

Declan groaned, scrubbed his hand over his face. "Is Jack with her?"

"She's alone. She didn't look like she'd be very comfortable in an interrogation room, so I had her wait in Saul's office. He's in a meeting and won't be back for a while."

Saul was the head marshal, and Eden hoped that his meeting involved something that would help them solve this case. He couldn't be pleased about several of his marshals being in the middle of a gunfight.

Harlan's phone buzzed, so he stepped away to his desk to take the call.

"I need you to see what you can do with these," Declan said, handing Clayton the envelope with the bank records.

Clayton glanced at them. Frowned. "Do I want to know where you got these?"

"From Eden's father, but I'm guessing he won't want to tell us his source."

"I'll get started on it," Clayton assured him. "You want me to tell Beatrice that your chat will have to wait? Neither of you look very steady on your feet right now."

"I'm not," Eden admitted. "But if she has information—"

"Not sure she does," Clayton interrupted. "She seems

a little off, if you ask me. Leonard might have been right about her being mentally unstable. The first thing she did when she got here was go into a rant about one of Kirby's lowlife brats causing her husband trouble."

Great. Just what they needed. Snobbish, jealous and perhaps crazy. As if they hadn't had enough of crazy for one day.

"What do we know about her?" Declan asked.

"She's fifty-eight and was first engaged to Jack over thirty years ago, but he broke off things to get engaged to Stella. Who then ended her engagement with Jack."

"For Kirby," Eden mumbled. "According to Leonard anyway. Is it true?"

"Still waiting for Stella to call back and confirm or deny it," Clayton explained. "But if it's true, Beatrice obviously made amends with Jack, and they've been married for going on thirty years. No kids. And they're rich. Very rich. It's his money, but she's half owner now. I'm still trying to get a handle on their net worth, but we're talking old money and plenty of it."

Eden glanced at the office where Beatrice was waiting. "I need a minute before we go in there and talk with her."

"You'll need more than a minute." Declan took her by the arm and led her down the hall to the break room. He shut the door and had her sit in one of the chairs. It wasn't exactly comfortable, more designed for someone having a quick bite or cup of coffee, but her legs were so wobbly that it was a relief just being off her feet.

"That call Harlan got could be about my father," she reminded him.

"And if it is, Harlan will come and tell us."

Since that was true, Eden stayed seated. Her thoughts were flying everywhere, probably because of the adrenaline pumping through her. But as bad as things were, and they were bad, she could only imagine how much worse it would be if she was going through it alone.

Declan took a bottle of water from the small fridge, opened it and had her take a sip. "Sorry that it's not something stronger." And it didn't sound as if he was joking.

Something stronger like a stiff drink was exactly what she needed. Or maybe not, she decided, when Declan dropped down next to her and eased his arm around her.

He definitely fell into the "something stronger" category.

"You can still see a doctor, you know," he offered.

"So can you. But I think we know a doctor won't have any fix for the shock of being shot at—again." She paused. "You'd think the second time would be easier. But it's not."

"If it got any easier, then it'd be time for me to turn in my badge. And for you to see a shrink. Nearly being killed should never feel *easier*."

Eden nodded. Groaned softly when she felt another slam of the fear. Her body was obviously still revved up for the fight that was over. Well, for now anyway. "My father—"

"Will be okay," Declan interrupted. "He had his men there, and if he's hurt, they'll get him the help he needs."

True. After all, they'd gotten him away from the scene, and there'd been no blood.

She looked at him, and even though there were dozens of things they could discuss about what had just happened, one of those whirlwind thoughts dropped from her head to her mouth. "My father thinks we're sleeping together."

"Yeah." He leaned in, brushed his lips over hers. Instant warmth. Or rather heat. Declan always seemed to know how to melt away the ice in her blood that the shooting had caused. "My brothers think that, too."

Eden groaned softly. "So we've been judged for something we haven't done."

"Yet," he added. The corner of his mouth lifted.

Ah, there it was. The killer smile to go along with those killer green eyes, rumpled black hair and perfect body. That helped, too. In fact, just being with him made things better. And that should have been a big red flag.

"Sleeping together won't help things," she reminded him. But then frowned because that didn't sound right. "Well, it might help with this ache, but it'll make our situation worse."

"There's an ache?" he asked.

She considered lying, but since the heat between them was past the sizzle stage, she'd only be wasting her breath. And speaking of breath, Declan pretty much robbed her of that when he leaned in and kissed her. Not one of those little lip touches he'd been giving her.

A real kiss.

She melted.

Like the rest of him, he was top-notch at that, too. His mouth moved over hers as if he wanted that ache to turn into something much more.

And it did.

The heat trickled through her. From her mouth to every inch of her. Especially the center of her body. A simple kiss had never been foreplay for her, but then a Declan kiss was far from simple.

With the water bottle still in her hand, Eden lifted her arms, first one and then the other, and she slipped them around his neck. The kiss deepened.

Everything did.

And they moved closer until they were touching breasts to chest. Until she wanted a whole lot more than she could have in the break room of the marshals' building.

"How's that ache now?" he said with his mouth still against hers.

Eden laughed. How that could happen, she didn't know. She could still hear the sound of those shots. Still see her father as he hit the ground. But somehow Declan had made her forget about it for a minute or two.

"I can't fall for you," she let him know.

He pulled back a little, pushed the hair from her face. "You already have."

Coming from any other man, that would have sounded cocky or even like a pick-up line, but Eden had to admit that it was true. She was falling for him. And that couldn't happen. She had to find a way to stop it, and she started by moving away from him.

It didn't help.

Even though they were no longer touching, she could still feel his hands on her. Could still taste him. And Eden knew she was well on her way to making what could turn out to be the biggest mistake of her life. Declan wasn't the sort of man she'd be able to just forget.

No.

He wasn't just inside her head now. He was edging his way into her heart. A far more dangerous place for him, considering in his eyes she'd always be her father's daughter.

"I'm tired of waiting," someone shouted from the hall. "I'll see Marshal O'Malley *now*."

That got Declan to his feet, and he moved Eden behind him. Protecting her again. But when he threw open the door, she wasn't so sure she needed his protection.

The woman coming toward them was tall but pencil thin. Hardly a physical threat.

Beatrice Vinson, no doubt.

She didn't look like a woman with mental problems, unless those problems included a serious high-end shopping addiction. She wore an expensive-looking creamy white cashmere skirt and matching sweater. No wrinkles anywhere on her face, and there wasn't any gray in her auburn hair. Her pale gray eyes went right to Declan.

"My husband came to see you." It sounded like an accusation of some kind.

Declan lifted his shoulder. "I questioned him about his possible involvement in a shooting. He's a suspect and, according to Leonard Kane, so are you."

The anger flashed through her eyes for just a second before she reined it in. "You're on a witch hunt. Probably on orders from Kirby Granger. Well, it won't do you any good. Neither my husband nor I had anything to do with these attacks."

"Then why are you here?" Eden asked.

Beatrice looked at her as if she were an insect to be swatted away. "You're Zander Gray's daughter, I assume."

Her icy gaze slid from Eden's head to her muddy shoes. She no doubt looked a wreck, felt like one, too, after Beatrice's scrutiny.

"The name says it all, doesn't it?" Beatrice added. "Your father's a criminal, and if Leonard didn't set all of this up, then Zander probably did." She paused. "I understand he's alive."

Declan jumped right on that. "How did you know?"

Beatrice dismissed that with the wave of her perfectly manicured hand. "I heard a rumor, but I'm not here to talk about Zander." Her gaze snapped to Declan. "I'm here to tell you to stop these ridiculous accusations about me and my husband. I don't care what the DNA test proves, you're not going to get one penny of my husband's money."

Eden had been following her. Until that last part. Declan was clearly confused, too, because he shook his head.

"Why would you think I'd want your money?" he demanded. "And what the hell does my DNA have to do with this?"

Now it was Beatrice's turn to look confused. Her fingers touched her parted lips.

"Stop!" someone called out.

Eden looked up the hall to see Stella frantically making her way toward Beatrice, Declan and her.

"Is something wrong with Kirby?" Declan immediately asked.

Stella was obviously too out of breath to answer right away, and she pressed her hand to her chest. However, her gaze went to Beatrice, and if looks could have killed, then Beatrice would be one dead woman.

"You had no right," Stella said to Beatrice.

Beatrice didn't back down. "Someone had to tell him the truth."

Declan went closer, nudging Beatrice aside, and he took Stella by the arm and led her into the break room. As he'd done earlier with Eden, he forced her to sit down.

"What's wrong?" Declan asked. "What's this all about?"

Stella and Beatrice looked at each other again. "If you don't tell him, I will," Beatrice threatened, her mouth in a tight red bud. "This ends right here, right now."

Eden glanced at Declan to see if he had any idea what was going on, but he didn't. He looked as dumbfounded as she did. Not Stella, though. The emotion was heavy in her eyes and face, but Eden couldn't tell what emotion it was exactly.

Stella looked up at Declan. "We have to talk. There are some things you need to know about your parents."

Chapter Twelve

A chill snaked down Declan's spine. He'd rarely seen Stella upset, but he was seeing it now. He was almost scared to guess what had put that look in her eyes.

Eden knew something was wrong, too, because she moved closer to him, taking his hand in hers.

"What about my parents?" Declan asked, and he tried to brace himself for an answer he was pretty sure he didn't want to hear.

Stella looked away from him. She kept her attention nailed to her hands in her lap, but he could have sworn she was blinking back tears.

"Tell him, Stella," Beatrice demanded.

Declan shot the woman a glare and was ready to toss her out of the building, but Stella finally looked up, met his gaze. He'd been right about those tears.

"I'm your birth mother," Stella whispered.

Declan shook his head, certain he'd misheard her. "You're *what?*"

"Your mother," Stella repeated.

Okay, so he hadn't misheard her after all, but it still took a moment to sink in. And when it did, those words came at him like a mountain being dropped on his head. The breath swooshed out of him, and because he had no choice, he leaned back against the doorjamb and let it support him.

"His mother?" Eden shook her head. "But his parents were killed in Germany when he was a boy."

"His adoptive parents were killed." Stella paused, blinked back more tears. "They were friends of friends with no link whatsoever to me. It had to be that way."

None of this made sense. "Why?" he managed to ask, and that one question could be about so many things. Declan didn't even know where to start.

"I'd just found out I was pregnant with you when someone tried to kill me," Stella continued. "I left the state. Tried to hide. But someone found me and attacked me again. That's when I left the country using a fake passport, and I gave birth to you in Germany."

Declan's head was pounding now. The thoughts flashing through them. The memories of his parents—meager memories, at that—were all lies. He wasn't the man he'd thought he was.

And Stella had spent decades lying to him.

He leaned down, still using the jamb for support, and he got right in her face. "Why didn't you tell me?"

"Because I was afraid someone would try to kill you." Despite the tears and shaky voice, she didn't hesitate. "The same person who tried to kill me."

"Someone killed my family," he reminded her, and he hated the anger in his voice. Stella was already on the verge of losing it. But he couldn't stop himself. Everything was crashing down on him.

Stella nodded. "I think they were murdered because someone was trying to get to you, because they found out you were my son. That's why you were sent to Ireland to be with Meg, a distant cousin of mine. But soon the threats started again, so I had you moved around from place to place."

"Until Meg dropped me off at Rocky Creek," Declan supplied.

"Yes." Stella paused again. "I arranged it after she couldn't handle the danger anymore. She was afraid she'd be murdered by the same person who'd killed your adoptive parents."

"Who killed them?" he shouted. Because he wanted them dead. That person had taken away everyone he'd loved, and had left him an orphan.

Or so he'd thought.

But his birth mother had been alive all along, and nearby the entire time he'd lived in Rocky Creek.

"Stella thinks I'm the one who tried to kill you," Beatrice volunteered.

Eden stepped between him and Beatrice, probably because she thought he might launch himself at the woman. "Why would she think that?"

But Beatrice didn't have to answer. Declan suddenly knew the reason why. "Because Jack Vinson is my biological father, and Beatrice was so insanely jealous that she wanted Stella and me dead."

That helped ease some of the, well, whatever the heck he was feeling for Stella. Anger, yes.

Maybe even rage.

And the feeling of being betrayed by someone he'd trusted. However, there was a bigger betrayal here, and she was standing right next to him wearing pricey clothes.

When Declan's glare landed on her, Beatrice actually dropped back a step, maybe because she saw that rage in him. She began to frantically shake her head.

"I didn't try to kill you. And I definitely didn't kill

your family. I wanted you out of my husband's life. Out of *my* life," she practically yelled. "You don't deserve to inherit anything *we* have."

"It's all about the money to her," Stella said in a whisper. "But until these attacks started and she showed up again, I had no idea she was behind them."

"I'm not!" Beatrice insisted.

Declan shut her out and motioned for Stella to continue. She was crying now, the tears streaking down her cheeks. "I thought the original attacks were from somebody that Kirby was investigating. He was dealing with some dangerous criminals in those days."

"Including Leonard Kane?" Eden asked.

Stella nodded. "This was about the same time that Kirby had to shoot and kill Leonard's son."

Declan's heart began to race even more than it already was, something he hadn't thought possible, since it felt as if his ribs were cracking. "Why would Leonard have gone after you?"

"Because he knew that Kirby loved her," Beatrice said before Stella could answer.

And Stella didn't deny it.

"I thought Jack Vinson could be behind the danger, too," Stella went on. "After all, I was engaged to him. And I cheated on him." That admission brought on more tears.

It also caused the room to go deadly silent.

Eden moved even closer to him. Slid her arm around his waist. Then they waited for Stella to finish. But that cheating confession was causing all sorts of thoughts to fly through his head.

"You cheated…with Kirby?" Declan asked.

"Who else?" Beatrice answered. "She never loved Jack. It was always about Kirby, and the moment she figured she could have him, she dropped Jack just like that." She snapped her fingers.

"You can leave now," Declan warned Beatrice, but he didn't take his attention off Stella. "Say it. I want to hear you say it."

Stella swallowed hard. "Kirby's your father."

Before he could stop it, a groan left his mouth, and even though Eden tried to hold on to him, he pushed her away.

Oh, man.

He hadn't seen this coming. Kirby was a good person. He'd saved him and his five foster brothers. But Stella and he had withheld the truth, and that cut Declan to the bone. To the very core of his soul.

"Kirby?" Beatrice looked at Stella as if she'd lost her mind. "You wish. You wanted your lover to be your baby's father, but we both know that Jack was."

"It was Kirby," Stella insisted. "I didn't tell him because I knew he'd probably end up getting killed trying to protect me and the baby. So after I gave birth to Declan in Germany, I left him with people I knew would give him a good, safe home. I thought I had covered my tracks." More tears came. "But obviously I hadn't."

"No, you hadn't." Declan wished he could cut her some slack. She was clearly hurting from all of this, but by God, the only family he'd known had been murdered.

"Does Kirby know now?" Eden asked.

Stella gave a shaky nod. "After Meg got sick, she called me to say she couldn't keep Declan any longer, so I arranged to have him brought to Rocky Creek. I told Kirby then."

Well, that explained why Kirby had taken such an interest in him. Except it hadn't felt like any more special treatment than he'd given the other boys who'd become his foster sons.

"Kirby wanted to tell you the truth," Stella went on, "but it was too dangerous. The threat was obviously still out there, and we didn't know who had killed your adoptive family. The safest thing for us to do was keep you close to us so we could watch out for you."

"So you changed his name?" Eden asked. "But he still had an Irish accent then. Didn't you think that'd make the killer suspicious?"

"The fear was always there, breathing down our necks," Stella verified. "But it wasn't as if we had a lot of choices. And besides, as far as the killer knew, Declan was in Germany somewhere, not Ireland. Then Kirby pointed out that the killer would think that Rocky Creek was the last place on earth we'd put our boy. Hiding him in plain sight, so to speak."

And it'd worked. He hadn't been free of Webb in those days, but a killer hadn't come after him.

There were so many questions that Declan wasn't sure where to start. "Someone left me a lot of money a while back, and I wasn't able to unravel where it came from."

"It was from me. It was my inheritance. I wanted you to have it, but I couldn't just give it to you, so I had it sent to you using a fake identity." She choked back a sob. "I swear, all these years, I was just trying to keep you safe."

"She's lying," Beatrice insisted. She pointed her finger at Declan. "I know you're Jack's son, and I know you want your hands on our money."

"My money," a man corrected.

Oh, man. It was Jack, and Declan didn't want to see him or anyone else right now.

Beatrice looked as if he'd slapped her, and she dropped back a step from him. "I didn't hear you come in."

"Obviously. Because you were too busy accusing Stella of lying." He walked closer, and his gaze connected with Stella's. "Is it true? Is Declan my son?"

Declan didn't realize he was holding his breath until his lungs started to ache.

Stella shook her head. "No. He's Kirby's. I got pregnant with him after you'd left on that business trip to Mexico."

Jack studied her. So did Declan. Beatrice just continued to mumble that Stella was lying.

"Why would I lie?" Stella challenged. "By admitting that Declan is Kirby's son, I'm not lessening the danger. I'm making it worse. And if I thought I had another choice, I'd take it. But despite everything I've done, I can't stop someone from trying to kill him."

Her voice broke, and she looked up at Declan. "I gave you up to save you."

He would have had to be an iceman not to react to that, and part of him wanted to pull her into his arms and say that he understood, but he couldn't do that. Not yet.

Maybe not ever.

Declan didn't say anything, couldn't, but Eden must have realized what he needed right now. She didn't waste any time moving both Jack and Beatrice aside. However, Eden did look back at Stella. "I'll call you later."

Maybe because she felt the pain that Stella was going through. Declan felt it, too, but he had to fight his way through all the other feelings first.

"Wait!" Jack called out. "I want to take a paternity test."

Declan didn't stop. He just kept moving. He had to get the hell out of there now.

"This isn't over," Jack added. "One way or another, I will learn the truth."

Yeah, so would Declan. After he came to grips with the world that'd just come crashing down hard around him.

Chapter Thirteen

Declan stormed out of the building so fast that Eden had a hard time keeping up with him. This had to be tearing him apart inside, yet he still gave their surroundings a lawman's glance before he got her into the parking lot and into his truck.

"I'm sorry," she said. The words were so useless, not nearly enough to help, but she wasn't sure anything would help right now.

Declan drove away fast, headed out of town and away from Stella. His mother. Even Eden was having trouble coming to terms with that, and she barely knew the woman. Or Kirby. But Kirby was also Declan's father.

If Stella had been telling the truth, that is.

Beatrice had been so adamant that she was lying, but as Stella had said—why would she lie about something that would ultimately only put Declan in more danger?

She wouldn't.

And that meant all these attempts on their lives were likely connected back to Kirby. It certainly made Leonard a stronger suspect. Of course, Beatrice had been very upset at the idea of sharing her husband's millions with a potential heir, so that gave her a serious motive to end Declan's life.

Without saying a word to her, Declan took out his

phone, and Eden saw from the name he pressed that he was calling Wyatt. His brother answered right away, and Declan pressed the speaker button and put the phone on the seat between them. Maybe because he had a white-knuckle grip on the steering wheel and didn't want to risk crushing the phone in his hand.

"I just talked to Stella," Wyatt said. "She's in pieces, Declan, and she's worried you'll do something reck-less. That was her word, not mine. I'm worried you'll do something stupid. Where are you?"

"With Eden. I need a favor." But he didn't continue for several long moments. "I need to know if Kirby's really my father."

"Already working on it. But even if it's true, you shouldn't be out there right now without backup. I don't have to remind you that someone wants you dead."

"No reminder needed. Let me know what you find out." And despite the fact that Wyatt was saying something, Declan hit the end call button.

It didn't take long, just seconds, for Wyatt to call back, but Declan silenced the ringer and put his phone on vibrate before he shoved it into his pocket. "I can't turn it off," he mumbled.

No, because they were in the middle of a complex investigation. One they couldn't put on hold, because she doubted these attempts to kill them would just end. Updates would be coming in. And possibly the culprit's capture.

Or so she hoped.

"Are you going to talk to Kirby?" she asked.

"I can't."

She understood, but she also knew it wasn't a conver-sation that Declan could delay for long. Kirby might have the answers they needed to blow this case wide open.

Of course, that would mean talking to Kirby about this bombshell that'd just been dropped on him.

Declan drove toward the ranch, but when he reached the fork in the road he stopped, as if trying to decide if he should go to his own place or the family home.

"The ranch has a security system," he finally said as if reminding himself, and he headed that way. "Once we're inside, I can get started on some calls. I need to find out if either Beatrice or Jack had any contacts in Germany at the time my family was killed. I also need to check their bank records to see if there's been any money siphoned off to pay for those gunmen."

"It can wait." Even if it shouldn't.

Declan didn't answer her. He brought the truck to a stop near the back door of the ranch, caught her hand and hurried her inside. They'd barely made it to the kitchen when he locked the door, engaged the security system and started making one of those calls.

However, Eden put her hand over his phone to stop him. "Want to talk about it first?"

She was certain he'd say no, but he groaned and leaned against the door. "I'm not sure how I'm supposed to deal with this."

Eden had to shake her head. "I don't know, either." But she pulled him into her arms and hoped that just the small gesture would help.

His heart was racing. She could feel it beating against her own chest. Could feel the tight muscles in his back and arms, too. He didn't say anything, but he leaned in, brushed a kiss on her forehead. Eden wasn't even sure he was aware he was doing it.

"I have a lot of questions." His voice was a whisper now. "But I don't think I can ask them yet."

She eased back just enough to meet his gaze. "You're angry with Stella and Kirby."

He nodded. But then shook his head. "I think I'm pissed off about everything."

"Well, for an angry man, you're doing a good job keeping it together."

"Poker face," he mumbled and tried to smile.

Eden didn't even try to return the smile or make light of this. His pain went bone deep, and it was going to take more than a few hours at home for him to come to terms with it.

He stared at her, pushed a strand of hair off her face. "How are you holding up?"

"Fine. I didn't just have my life turned upside down."

"No, but you had bullets fired at you."

It was strange that she could push something like that aside. She certainly wasn't accustomed to having people try to kill her, or her father caught in the middle of an attack, and she prayed it never became routine. But it wasn't routine for her to see Declan hurting like this, either.

He leaned in again. Kissed her. It had no trace of the dark emotions that had to be boiling inside him. No trace of anything but a simple, sweet kiss.

And then it wasn't so sweet.

Declan made a sound. A groan of pain that came from deep within his chest. He eased his hand around the back of her neck, urged her closer and kissed her until Eden's legs felt wobbly. Until the heat seeped through every inch of her.

But this was wrong.

The kiss was past being good. Declan's always were, and she was getting maximum benefit from his mouth on hers. But it felt as if she was taking advantage of him.

He was in a very bad place, and the kisses he was using to shatter her into a thousand little pieces were kisses he was using to try to deal with the pain.

Better than punching something.

Not better, though, than trying to deal with it.

Still, he didn't stop and neither did she. Eden just let herself dissolve into his arms and let his mouth take her to the only place she wanted to go.

Eden heard the buzzing sound, and for a moment she thought it was part of the heat firing through her body. But then Declan cursed, took out his vibrating phone and she saw the screen lit up with a call from Unknown.

"Marshal O'Malley," Declan answered, caution in his voice, and he hit the speaker button.

"It's me, Zander. I need to speak to my daughter."

The relief was instant. But short-lived. "Are you all right? Were you shot?" she asked.

"I'm okay. I was wearing a bulletproof vest. It saved my life. Now, I need to know what the hell is going on. Who's trying to kill us?"

"We're not sure," Eden said.

Declan picked up where she left off. "We're still investigating it, but I haven't taken you off my suspect list."

"Well, you damn well should," her father insisted. "I was nearly killed today, and if that bullet had hit me in the head instead of the chest, I'd be a dead man. I'm not stupid, and I wouldn't have set up a fake attack that could have killed me and my daughter."

Declan only gave a heavy sigh, and she couldn't tell if he believed him or not. "Where are you? You need to turn yourself in."

"I will. I just need a little more time to prove my innocence. Did you find out anything useful with those bank records I gave you?"

"Nothing so far, except that they can't be used because they were illegally obtained. How'd you get them?"

"You wouldn't believe me if I told you." Her father mumbled something she couldn't understand. "Someone sent them to me. And I don't know who. The package didn't have a postmark and was left with a friend who knew how to get in touch with me in case of an emergency."

It hurt to know that he'd trusted someone else and not her in case of an emergency, but Eden wanted to give him the benefit of the doubt. Her father might have thought the marshals would have her phone tapped.

And they might have.

It would have been too risky for him to contact her.

"Keep looking for something. Anything," her father added. "And keep Eden locked inside wherever it's safe."

She wasn't sure such a place existed. Their attacker seemed to have a lot more information about them than they did him or her.

Her father hung up, but Declan didn't put his phone away. He scrolled through the numbers to call Clayton.

"People are worried about you," Clayton greeted. "Me included."

"I just need a little downtime," Declan said. He glanced at her mouth, and she wondered if the kiss had been just that. Downtime. An outlet for all that dangerous energy brewing inside him.

It'd be easier if it were.

But this attraction, for Eden, was the real deal. That didn't make it easier, but it did leave open the possibility that she'd walk away from this with a severely broken heart.

"Zander just called about those bank statements." Declan brushed a kiss on her cheek, stepped away from her.

Even from the other end of the line, she could hear Clayton take a deep breath. Maybe because he wanted to discuss his brother's well-being rather than the case. "The records seem to prove Leonard Kane took out a large sum of money from his offshore account around the same time someone tried to kill that witness who'd testified against Zander Gray."

The witness her father had been accused of trying to kill. But the problem was, this couldn't be used to prove anything. In fact, Leonard himself could have sent the records just as a way of adding some mental torture to this already torturous situation.

"The most recent records indicate that Leonard might be doing the same now," Clayton went on. "He transferred about a quarter of a million just a week ago."

"About the time someone was planning to hack into Eden's computer," Declan provided.

Oh, mercy. A quarter of a million could buy a lot of hired guns and bribe plenty of people to get whatever information he needed. But then, maybe someone was setting up Leonard.

Like Beatrice or Jack.

"Since we can't use the records, we'll have to try to find where the money was spent." Declan checked the clock on the wall. "I'll be there in about twenty minutes."

"No, you won't. Saul's orders. He told me to tell you to stay away from the office for the rest of the day."

Declan closed his eyes a moment. Not from relief. She could see the frustration all over his face. "I need to be there working."

"No, you need to be guarding Eden. Saul's put her in your protective custody."

Eden wasn't exactly surprised by that. She needed some kind of protection, and Declan was her best bet for that. But it did make her wonder if Declan's boss had heard rumors of the attraction simmering between them. Declan's brothers had certainly picked up on it.

"There's more," Clayton said a moment later. "Wyatt's working on your, well, paternity, but one of the first things that popped up was that Beatrice took a trip to Germany." He paused. "Declan, it was right around the time your family was killed."

"Hell." Declan added even more profanity and would have stormed back outside if Eden hadn't stepped in front of him.

"Any evidence that Beatrice hired someone to kill them?" Eden asked.

"None. In fact, Jack has her on a fairly tight personal budget because she tends to go through money like water. We're following the money trail she left when she was there, but her visit might have had nothing to do with the murders."

"Then why was she there, damn it?" Declan snapped.

"That's something I'll find out. And note that I said *I* and not *us*. That's because I've got to distance you from this. I don't want anything incriminating that we might find tossed out because the D.A. thinks we manufactured evidence."

The muscles in Declan's jaw stirred, and for a moment she thought he still might refuse, that he might head to the marshals' building anyway. However, he didn't reach to disarm the security system or open the door.

"Find something we can use," he told Clayton. "I'll

see what I can come up with without using official resources."

Declan hung up and started out of the room, probably
to work on something he wasn't ready to do. "I'll pour
you a drink," Eden offered.

The kitchen was huge, with over a dozen cabinets,
and she waited a moment, hoping that he'd point her in
the right direction for that drink. But he didn't. Declan
just stared at her.

"I'm sorry about this," he said. "But you're a better
fix than a drink."

And that was the only warning he gave her before
he snapped her to him and kissed her again. Not a gentle one this time. This was all heat and nerves. Mostly
nerves. But like his other kisses, it was still strong stuff.
The man knew how to light every fire in her body with
just his mouth.

He deepened the kiss. His grip on her got tighter. The
emotion upped a notch, something she hadn't thought
possible. So did the need that his kiss was building inside her.

But then he stopped, looked down at her. "I'm sorry
for this, too."

She shook her head, not understanding, but he came
right back to her for a kiss of a different kind. No nerves.

Just the heat.

Oh, she got it then. He was sorry that this was turning into something that neither of them seemed to be
emotionally ready for. Or able to stop.

Eden certainly couldn't.

She kissed him right back, and when he turned, pressing her against the counter, she pulled him right along
with her. Until his body was pressed against hers. Until
every inch of them was touching.

"You should say no," he reminded her, her mouth still against her.

"You should, too," she repeated to him.

But he kissed her again, and all reminders went right out the window.

"Whatever sympathy or pity you're feeling for me, it shouldn't play into this," he snarled.

Even though she had to break the kiss to do it, she looked him straight in the eye. "What I feel for you doesn't have anything to do with sympathy." She slid her hand over the front of his jeans, felt him hard and ready. "And apparently it doesn't for you, either."

He cursed again and looked as if he was in the middle of a serious mental debate. "I knew you were trouble when I first saw you. Too bad I really like this kind of trouble."

Well, good. Because it was all she could offer him now. Trouble and scalding-hot kisses. A bad combination, but it beat feeling the pressure from the danger and the investigation. Heck, this beat anything and everything she'd experienced.

His hand left her waist and slid beneath her shirt. He lit some little fires along the way as his fingers trailed up from her stomach to her breasts. His touch was like his kiss. Magic. And Eden knew this was going to lead them straight to the bed—or the floor—if she didn't stop it.

But she didn't want to stop.

And while Declan touched her and gave her another of those scalding kisses, she considered just how good this would be.

Bad, of course, too.

Because they didn't have time for sex and the aftermath it would create, and there would be an aftermath.

It would only deepen her feelings for a man who could ultimately destroy her father.

Or vice versa.

Besides, Declan would regret this. Maybe not today but eventually. And it was that reminder that gave her just enough strength to step back.

He let her slip from his arms, her top dropping back into place. But her breathing didn't level, and the burning need inside her didn't go away, either. Eden just stood there, waiting to see how long this puny dose of strength was going to last.

Probably not very long.

She wanted him more than all the rational reasons she could come up with for keeping out of his arms.

Declan's phone buzzed again, the soft sound shooting through the room. "Wyatt," he said, glancing at the screen. He looked at Eden as if debating if he should answer it and knowing he had no choice but to talk to his brother.

"No need to check up on me," Declan greeted him and put the call on speaker.

"Glad to hear it, 'cause I had plans to do that, but we got a problem. I'm leaving now to deal with a hostage situation over in Eagle Pass. But I just got a call from the deputy we have guarding Kirby's room."

"What happened?" Declan snapped.

Eden held her breath. Prayed. This had already been a hellish day without adding more.

"Leonard Kane just showed up and demanded to see Kirby," Wyatt explained. "And before Stella could call me to tell me what was going on, Kirby let Leonard into his room so they could *talk*. Little brother, you need to get over there fast."

Chapter Fourteen

Declan flew into the hospital parking lot, and as soon as he brought his truck to a stop, he barreled out. He did wait though for Eden to exit and hurry to his side. And he also glanced around to make sure this wasn't all some kind of setup for another attack.

Everything looked normal.

But it wouldn't stay that way. Not with Leonard and Kirby in the same room.

"If he hurts Kirby, Leonard's a dead man," Declan said under his breath.

Yeah, he was riled to the core that Kirby hadn't told him about being his father, but he owed Kirby a lot. His life, in fact, and there was no way he was going to let Leonard ride roughshod over a man too weak to fight back.

"The deputy wouldn't let Leonard do anything stupid," Eden reminded him.

It was a good reminder. The deputy was there. But Leonard was a man hell-bent on revenge because Kirby had shot and killed his son all those years ago. If Leonard had murder on his mind, he probably wouldn't let a deputy stop him.

Or Stella.

In fact, Leonard could kill all of them.

Declan hurried toward the side exit, and as on their previous visit, he maneuvered Eden through the halls to Kirby's room. The first sign of trouble he saw was the deputy standing outside Kirby's closed door. The deputy had his gun drawn, but he wasn't inside where he needed to be to protect Kirby and Stella.

"Why aren't you in there?" Declan shouted.

"Kirby's orders. He said he and his visitor needed to have a private discussion. Leonard agreed. He had his men go to the cafeteria to wait. Kirby sent Stella to Doc Landry's office and told her to stay there with the door locked. The hospital security guard's with her."

And that meant no one was with Kirby, protecting him.

Declan didn't even bother to hold back the profanity, but he did push Eden behind him and draw his gun. The deputy stepped aside so that Declan could throw open the door to Kirby's room.

He braced himself to see a fight, but Kirby was in his bed, sitting up and looking stronger than he had in weeks. Leonard was standing next to him and had no weapon. At least not a visible one.

"Get away from him," Declan insisted.

Leonard smiled, but there was no humor in it. "I'm here at Kirby's invitation."

Kirby nodded. "He is. I wanted to talk to him, to try to settle this old score between us."

"But it's a score that can't be settled," Leonard argued.

"You shouldn't be talking to this snake," Declan insisted. He tried to stay in front of Eden, but she stepped out and went closer to Kirby.

"Maybe this meeting can wait until you're stronger," Eden suggested softly to Kirby.

Kirby reached out, took her hand in his. "That's a kindness I don't deserve from you. Or you," he added, his gaze going to Declan. "Saying I'm sorry won't help, but I'm saying it anyway."

Declan glanced at Leonard to see if he knew anything about what this conversation meant. Judging from the smug look he got, he did.

"Yeah, I know he's your daddy," Leonard confirmed. "Some things started popping up a few weeks ago."

"Someone tried to run your DNA," Kirby explained. "I put a stop to it, but not before Leonard got his hands on it."

"Who ran his DNA?" Eden asked.

Declan wanted to know the same damn thing, but Kirby only shook his head. "I figured it was Leonard here, but he says no."

Leonard held up his hands, palms out. "Wasn't me. But Kirby thought that maybe it was the first step to me getting payment for what happened to my boy, Corey."

Kirby made a weary sigh, and he let go of Eden's hand. "I had no choice but to shoot Corey. Somewhere, deep down in your ice-cold heart, you know that. And you also know that trying to settle this score with Declan is just plain wrong. He had no part in Corey's death. No choice in fathers, either."

It was true. And ironic. Declan used to wish that Kirby was his real father. Now it was true, and he just couldn't get past the lies he'd been fed.

"Why didn't you tell me?" Declan came out and asked.

"I didn't know at first, not until Stella spilled everything after you'd arrived at Rocky Creek. Then, when I found out that someone might want you dead because of me, I couldn't risk telling you."

"You could have sent me away," Declan pointed out.

"Could have." Kirby paused after that agreement. "But I didn't figure that'd be any safer than having you in my sights. Of course, it meant you having to deal with that SOB, Jonah Webb."

Yeah, that'd been no picnic. Declan had gotten beatings from Webb, but now, looking back on it, he would have gotten a heck of a lot more if it hadn't been for Stella, and even Kirby, intervening.

"After I realized what Webb was doing and that I couldn't stop him, I tried just about everything I could to get you out of Rocky Creek," Kirby went on, "but I couldn't do it out in the open. Couldn't let anyone make the connection that you were my son."

And maybe that was why Kirby had fostered not just him but the boys who'd become his brothers. But Declan had to amend that. Whatever Kirby's reasons were for getting them out, there'd been no shortage of love and fatherly guidance before and after he'd taken them into foster care.

Kirby drew in a long breath, and he kept his gaze locked with Declan's. "But now the danger's back. Everything that Stella and I did to protect you wasn't enough. That's why I asked Leonard to come. If he feels the need for revenge, I want him to take it out on me. Not you."

"No." Declan charged forward, shoving Leonard aside. "You're not killing him."

Leonard stayed put and turned his glare on Declan. "Don't get your jeans in a twist. Killing Kirby is the last thing I want. It'll end his suffering too soon. It'll end this." He motioned first to Declan, then Kirby. "And as far as I can tell, I want *this*. Because it's clear that you and Kirby are at odds over his daddy lie."

Eden folded her arms over her chest. "Are you saying you don't want us dead?"

"No. I'm saying I don't want you dead *right now*." Leonard's gaze shifted to Declan. "And if you think you can use that to arrest me, think again, honey bun. Wishing you dead and doing something about it are two different things."

Declan couldn't argue with that. Still, he'd look for an excuse, any excuse, to slap this moron behind bars.

"The way I got it figured, Declan can put Kirby through a lot more pain and suffering than I can by putting a bullet in his blood kin," Leonard added. "Or a bullet in an old business partner's blood kin."

Eden's father. And since Leonard smiled when he said it, Declan figured Leonard still had a lot of ill will toward Zander. On this point, the feeling was mutual. At least it had been until today, but he was beginning to have serious doubts about Zander's guilt.

"So this feud is over?" Eden asked.

"Postponed," Leonard clarified. He winced a little, touched his fingers to his temple. "Of course, it can't be postponed for too long. I got my own deathbed to deal with."

Yeah, and Declan needed answers before that happened, because he had the sick feeling that Leonard had already made arrangements that would extend beyond his grave.

Arrangements to kill all of them.

"I know you hired someone to try to kill the witness scheduled to testify against Zander," Declan said. It wasn't exactly a bluff. He did know it, had the bank records that all but proved it, but he couldn't *prove* it in a court of law. Still, he wanted to see Leonard's reaction. "You did that to set Zander up for murder. A different kind of score to settle, huh?"

Leonard didn't respond other than to slide his fingers around the metal footboard on Kirby's bed. He certainly didn't deny it.

"Now you've hired more gunmen. More killers," Declan spelled out. "I want names so I can put a stop to this."

His demand undoubtedly would fall on deaf ears, but Declan had to try. And this time he did get a reaction. "I didn't hire anyone."

A lie, probably. But the look on Leonard's face seemed real. He went ashy pale, sweat popping out on his forehead, and his grip tightened on the footboard.

"Get a doctor in here now," Leonard said, his voice punctuated with his suddenly shallow breathing.

Eden obviously thought he wasn't faking it because she pressed the button on the wall next to Kirby's bed.

"Don't worry." Leonard's color was even worse now. So was his breathing. "I'm not ready to croak yet. Kirby and I still have some unfinished business."

With that threat still hanging in the air, the door opened and a nurse rushed in.

"I got a terminal, inoperable brain tumor," Leonard managed to say to her.

The nurse looked at Leonard, hurried to him and called for assistance. It didn't take long before the room was a flurry of activity. Another nurse and a medic came rushing in with a wheelchair, and the trio helped Leonard into it before they whisked him away.

Kirby still didn't lie down, but Eden adjusted his pillows and eased him back. "I can wait outside while you two talk," she offered.

Both Kirby and Declan shook their heads. "You need to stay here with me," Declan said, and it wasn't a suggestion. She wasn't leaving his sight because all of this could be a ploy by Leonard to separate them. Especially since Leonard would know that Kirby and Declan had to *talk*.

"I don't want pity playing into this," Kirby said, looking at Declan. "You need to go ahead and get it out. Blast me for what I did."

Declan wanted to do just that. He wanted this firestorm of feelings to go away and for things to go back to how they were. But that was impossible. He was looking at his birth father. A man who might be dying. So, yeah, pity would play into this. Worry and fear, too. There was no way he could blast Kirby while he was in this condition.

"I wish I'd known," Declan settled for saying. He reholstered his gun.

"I wish I'd been able to tell you. Just know I was always proud of you. Always loved you."

Declan hadn't doubted that, and he didn't doubt that Kirby loved his foster brothers equally.

"Don't put any of this on Stella," Kirby continued. "She was scared spitless for you, and she gave you up to make sure you'd live. That makes her a saint in my book."

"You still love her," Eden said under her breath.

But Kirby didn't have time to confirm or deny that. There were some voices in the hall, and a moment later someone appeared in the still-open doorway.

Declan drew his gun again.

As Beatrice stepped into the room.

She didn't step in easily. The deputy had hold of her arm, trying to haul her back, and despite the arctic glare she was giving him, he didn't let go.

"I have to speak to you." Her glare snapped to Declan. "Tell your Neanderthal to back off before I slap him with a lawsuit."

Declan didn't care if she sued or not, and he was about to tell the deputy to toss her out on her designer-clad butt.

"I have proof that Kirby's not your father," Beatrice snarled.

That stopped Declan from giving the toss-her-out order, and the moment the deputy's grip eased off her, Beatrice came storming toward him. She wasn't armed, but she did have a piece of paper in her hand. She thrust it toward him.

"It's the results of a DNA test I had run on you," she explained.

Declan didn't look at the paper yet. "How the hell did you get my DNA?"

Her chin came up. "I had someone take it from a cup you used at the diner across the street."

That seemed like a lot of trouble to go through, but then Beatrice was worried about his paternity.

"I had your DNA compared to Jack's, and it's a match," she continued. "That doesn't mean you have a right to our money. I checked, and since Kirby adopted you, that'll make it next to impossible for you to try to make any claims against Jack's estate."

Declan looked at the results. It was a standard lab test that he was used to reading, but he wasn't used to seeing his name associated with someone else who was supposed to be his biological father.

"The test results are fake," Kirby said. He met Beatrice's gaze. "I'm Declan's father, so there's no reason for Jack or you to come after him."

Beatrice shook her head. "I had the result tested at a reputable lab."

"BioMedical," Kirby provided. "I have a lot of friends in this field. Law enforcement, too. And I had flags put on Declan's name in case anyone tried to have his DNA tested. The lab called this morning and said there'd been a mix-up and the results had been released to you."

"The real results?" someone asked from the doorway. It was Jack.

Both Declan and Eden groaned. This meeting was already complicated enough without adding a paternity candidate to it.

"Beatrice got fake results," Kirby insisted. "I had a DNA test done years ago. One that I know wasn't tampered with, and Declan's my son."

Declan braced himself for Jack's denial, but the man only lifted a piece of paper that he was holding. "I heard Beatrice making arrangements for the DNA test, and I paid a lab tech to do a second test and give me the results." He walked closer, handed the paper to Declan.

"You what?" Beatrice snapped. "You went behind my back?"

Jack's eyes darkened. "You went behind mine."

That brought on an argument as to which one of them had done the right thing, but Declan tuned them out. Eden obviously did, too, because she looked at both the papers with him.

Hell.

What was this about?

"How can this be?" Eden asked, and her voice was loud enough to stop the Vinsons' argument. Both Jack and Beatrice turned to Declan and her.

Declan lifted the paper that Beatrice had given him. "This test claims that Jack is my biological father." He lifted the other one. "And the one that Jack gave me says that Kirby is."

Jack came closer, snatched the papers from Declan's hands and looked at them. He cursed. "Is this some kind of joke?"

"No joke," Kirby answered. "I didn't pay the tech to falsify the result, only to alert me that a DNA test had been ordered so I could do some damage control."

Beatrice had a look at the papers as well, and she looked as confused as her husband. "Who would have done this? And what's the truth?"

"I've already told you the truth," Kirby continued. "Declan is mine. Now, I know that makes him a target in Jack's eyes. He might want to eliminate him to get back at Stella and me—"

"I don't want to eliminate anyone," Jack snapped. "I just want the truth."

Kirby looked him straight in the eye. "He's my son, not yours." His gaze shifted to Beatrice. "And that gives you no motive for murder."

Beatrice gasped as if insulted that he would accuse her of such a thing, but she sure didn't deny it. She did, however, look at the papers again. "Who would have faked the DNA-test results?"

"Someone who wanted to incite you to kill Declan." Kirby's attention shifted to Jack. "And that's the same reason you got the real results. That gives both of you motives to try to kill him."

It was true. But the problem was, who had created the fakes? Either of them could have, whether to draw suspicion off themselves, or in Jack's case, maybe he wanted his wife to commit murder. Better than a divorce, where he'd have to split his assets with her. Of course, Beatrice could have faked the results to do the same to Jack. With Jack behind bars for murder, she'd have control of all the money.

So they were back to square one.

"I won't let either of you hurt him," Kirby said. And before Declan realized what he was doing, Kirby reached beneath his pillow and drew his gun.

He pointed it right at Jack.

Kirby's eyes narrowed, too. "I think it's time for you to confess everything you know about these attacks."

"I know nothing about them." Jack's hand moved toward his jacket, but Declan turned his own gun in the man's direction.

"I wouldn't do that if I were you," Declan warned him. "Nerves are a little bit raw right now." He glanced at Kirby. "Yours, too. Why don't you put that gun away and let me handle this."

But Kirby obviously didn't listen. He turned that frosty glare on Beatrice. "Start talking."

She frantically shook her head. "I don't know anything. I'm certainly not responsible for what's going on with your son." Beatrice made that particular label sound like a disease. "And I'm leaving. I won't stand here and be subjected to the likes of you."

Beatrice turned and walked out, practically knocking the deputy off balance. Declan was sure she'd actually left because he heard her heels clacking on the tile floor.

"You should go, too," Declan warned Jack.

Jack's mouth tightened, and he mumbled something Declan didn't catch before he, too, stormed out.

"You need to get Clayton on this," Kirby said the moment Jack was out of the room. He released a long, labored breath.

All of his foster brothers were already neck deep in this case and their regular investigations. Added to that, his sisters-in-law's lives were on hold because they couldn't return to the ranch until it was safe. At the rate they were going, that might never happen.

"More trouble?" Stella said from the doorway. She gave both Declan and Eden a concerned glance, but most of her concern was for Kirby. And he needed it. Kirby looked weaker than ever, and Stella went to him.

"Guess it won't do any good to say you shouldn't have had these meetings," she scolded him. Stella took the water glass from the stand and made Kirby take a sip.

Declan saw it then. The affection between the two. Maybe even the love.

Why hadn't he seen it earlier?

Maybe because he'd been too wrapped up in his own life and Kirby's illness. Now he was wrapped up in keeping Eden and himself alive. Kirby and Stella, too, because despite Kirby's warning, Declan figured Jack, Beatrice and even Leonard could all come back.

Declan walked closer to the deputy. "I need you to call the sheriff and have him beef up security here at the hospital. I don't want the Vinsons or Leonard Kane allowed back in the building, much less anywhere near Kirby."

The deputy nodded and took out his phone to make the call just as Declan's own cell buzzed. He glanced at the screen and saw the caller was Unknown again.

"I think it's your father," he relayed to Eden, and that sent her hurrying across the room toward him.

Declan answered the call and put it on speaker.

"O'Malley, I want you to take Eden someplace safe and keep her there until this is over."

Yeah, it was her father all right, and he sounded out of breath. As if he was running. Or chasing someone.

"What's wrong?" Declan asked.

"Something's finally right. I know who's trying to kill you, and I'm going to stop it. This ends *now*."

And with that, Zander hung up.

Chapter Fifteen

The waiting and not knowing were getting to her. By now, Eden figured she should be accustomed to both, but she obviously wasn't. She felt raw. Like one big giant nerve.

Nothing felt safe. Not even the ranch, though Declan had asked the hands to arm themselves and be on the lookout for anyone suspicious. It was only after those measures that Declan had brought her to wait for her father's call or any other update they could get on the case.

So far, they'd had zero in either department.

No more calls from her father. No breaks in the investigation. So they were in wait-and-worry mode. Well, she was anyway. Declan had disappeared into another part of the house just minutes earlier, so maybe he'd found something productive to do.

Not her, though. Unless pacing qualified as productive.

She was tired of pacing. Tired of the feeling of panic crawling over her. But she was afraid to sit for fear the exhaustion would take over and she'd collapse. That was the last thing Declan needed after everything he'd been through today.

And what they still had to face.

Maybe her father could fix this and put an end to the

danger. She prayed that was possible. But she didn't want that at the expense of his life. She had enough emotions to deal with without adding grief and guilt.

Speaking of guilt, she heard another sound of it coming her way. Declan. A guilty feeling of a different kind. Eden turned and spotted him making his way into the family room. He'd taken off his jacket, but still had on his holster over a great-fitting plain white T-shirt.

Mercy.

The man could make something that simple look good, along with helping some of the tension slide right from her body.

His walk was a swagger. Natural, no doubt, and his nondesigner jeans fit him like a glove. He had a drink in his left hand and was sipping from another in his right.

"You need this," he said, handing her the glass.

Even though Eden wasn't much of a drinker, she took a sip anyway, and the cool whiskey burned her throat all the way down.

Declan took another gulp of what appeared to be a quadruple shot. Apparently, he needed it, too. And he tipped his head to the stairs. "It's getting late. Why don't you get some rest and I'll keep watch."

The prospect was tempting, especially since the security system was on and there were a half dozen ranch hands guarding the place.

"Why don't we both rest," she suggested. The next sip of whiskey went straight to her head. Or maybe that was just Declan's doing. The man was potent stuff.

The corner of his mouth lifted. "If we rest together, it won't be restful."

True. And while that would complicate the heck out of both of their lives, it was tempting. Even more so when he leaned in and brushed one of those mind-numbing kisses on her lips. However, he didn't carry it any further. He just lit that particular fire, stepped away and leaned against the wall, facing her.

That didn't help, either.

He was drop-dead hot, and it didn't matter how bad their situation got. He was still drop-dead hot.

"Your father wouldn't approve anyway," Declan said, as if trying to talk himself out of whatever he was feeling.

And what was he feeling?

Eden realized they'd yet to talk about something so, well, normal. It'd all been criminal reports, interviews with suspects and dodging bullets. Hardly the right atmosphere for talking about what was going on inside their hearts. But there was a lot going on inside hers.

"My father definitely wouldn't approve," she agreed. "But he's never had a say in my personal life."

His eyebrow lifted. "With the way you defend him, I thought you were close."

"No. It's complicated." But then she laughed. "Something you know a little about."

"Yeah." He groaned and sank to the floor, his back still against the wall.

Even though it was a dangerous move, Eden went closer, stooped and sat down beside him. "Want to talk about Kirby and Stella?"

He stayed quiet for so long that Eden was certain he would say no. But he had another large sip of his whiskey. "I want to hate them, but I can't. Because I've thought of Kirby as my father for a long time now."

"And Stella?"

Declan lifted his shoulder and set his whiskey glass on the floor. "I remember her looking out for me at Rocky Creek. Once, Jonah Webb, the headmaster, was giving me a beating, and Stella stepped in and stopped it. She nearly got fired. After that, she always tried to keep herself between me and Webb. Sometimes, she succeeded."

It crushed her heart to hear what he'd been through at that horrible place. She'd read accounts of it, but nothing in those accounts told her of the physical abuse Declan had gone through.

"Don't." He leaned in, gave her another of those idle kisses. "No need to feel sorry for me. All of that happened a long time ago."

"It's the reason you became a marshal."

He nodded. "That and Kirby." He didn't kiss her, but he did run his thumb over her bottom lip and then brought it to his own mouth to taste.

Her stomach did a serious flip-flop.

He didn't make a move to turn that into a real kiss, so Eden did. She moved in on him, pressing her mouth to his and sliding her hand around the back of his neck.

Declan made a sound. Part groan, part grunt. But he didn't push her away. Nope. He hauled her to him and kissed her until all the nerves were gone. Well, the regular nerves. The heat and the sensations of pleasure were right there, urging her on.

But he didn't urge her for long. Declan eased back. Stared at her. "If I take you now, you'll regret it."

"You're sure? Because this doesn't feel like regret."

He chuckled. Like the rest of him, that was hot, too. Of course, in the state she was in, his breathing was a turn-on.

"Do you have any idea what you do to me?" she asked.

"Yeah. You do the same to me. That's why you'll take a shower alone. Clear your head. Then we can…talk if you're still feeling up to it."

He was giving her an out. An out Eden wasn't sure she wanted. But it was something he insisted on, because he got to his feet and helped her to hers.

Another kiss. Much too quick. And he put his hand on the small of her back to get her moving up the stairs. "I'll make some calls and see if anyone has any news."

That couldn't hurt, but she figured if there truly was news, someone would have already called. He led her to the guest room, where she'd stayed the night before. It was just up the hall from his. Two doors down.

But he didn't head there.

He waited in the doorway of her room, watching her. And she would have been blind not to see the heat in his eyes.

"You're sure I need some time?" she asked.

He smiled again. That slow, lazy smile that turned her to liquid fire. "I'm trying to be a gentleman here."

The seconds passed, slowly. His smile went south. And he pushed himself away from the doorjamb.

"But then we both know I'm not a gentleman," he drawled.

DECLAN CAME TOWARD her and hauled her into his arms.

He figured this was a few steps past stupid, but that didn't stop him. In fact, it'd take Eden telling him no to stop, and she definitely didn't say no. She pulled him closer and made a sound of what appeared to be relief. Declan totally got that. Eden and he had been skirting each other for two days now, and this blasted attraction had reached a boiling point.

One touch of his mouth to hers and the boiling point seemed cool compared to what he was feeling inside. It'd been a while since he'd wanted a woman this much, and in the back of his mind, he knew that was a lie. He'd *never* wanted anyone this much, even if she was the very woman he should be backing away from.

And maybe that was the bottom line here.

This was forbidden, and maybe that made it feel so damn necessary. And so much hotter.

He kissed her hard. Too hard. And while they fought to get closer, they off balanced themselves and darn near fell on their butts. All in all, the floor wouldn't have been a bad place to be, but he needed to get to his room, where he had some condoms. He didn't want to double his trouble by having unprotected sex. Protected sex was going to be memorable enough. And apparently inevitable.

Without breaking the kiss, Declan maneuvered Eden out of the guest room and in the direction of his room.

"You'd better not stop," she said against his mouth.

He wouldn't stop. Common sense was out the window now, and he was in take-her-now mode. Worse, Eden was in the same take-me frame of mind, so Declan figured he stood no chance of slowing this down. He got her inside his bedroom and kicked the door shut.

She went after his T-shirt, only to curse the holster that got in the way. Declan helped her with that, dropping the gun and holster on the nightstand, and they tumbled onto the bed. The feather mattress swelled up on both sides of them, cocooning them, and with one swift move, Eden was on top of him, straddling him.

Her eyes were wild and hot. Like the rest of her. And she finally got his T-shirt off and sent it sailing across the room. Now she slowed a little. Her gaze slid over his bare chest.

"No," she mumbled.

Declan glanced down to see what'd prompted that, and her attention was on the four-inch scar on the side of his chest. But only briefly. Her gaze went from the scar to the rest of him, including his stomach and lower, to the zipper of his jeans.

"No?" he asked.

"Not that kind of no," Eden quickly clarified. "No as in I was hoping your body wasn't as good as my imagination thought it'd be. But you're better than anything I could have imagined."

He was flattered. And confused. "So why the no?"

"Because with a body like yours, you're used to *wow*, and I don't have a wow kind of body."

Declan seriously doubted that. The woman burned him to ash, and he figured whatever was beneath those clothes would only make the burn faster and hotter.

So he did something to prove it.

Declan stripped off her top. And he gave her the same once-over she'd given him. She was wearing a bra, white and no frills, and he unclasped the front hook and rid her of that, too. Her breasts spilled into his hands.

Man, she was perfect.

But while he was gawking, he unzipped her jeans and shimmied them off her. The panties matched the bra. Nothing special, but when he removed those, the woman beneath still fell into that perfect category.

"You'll do just fine," he teased, and he pulled her down to him so he could kiss her the way he wanted.

First, her mouth.

Then he shifted their positions and went exploring. To the curve of her neck. He got a good response there. A nice little breathy moan. Then he went to her breasts and took her right nipple into his mouth.

Better-than-nice response.

The moan was louder, and she arched her back to give him more of her. He stayed there for several moments. Pleasuring her and pleasuring himself. Before he dropped some kisses on her stomach.

He took in her scent. Her sex. And coupled with the kissing, he was burning for her when she caught him and flipped their positions.

"I want these off now," Eden said, and she tackled the zipper on his jeans.

Yeah, he wanted that, too, but after she fumbled with the zipper, trying to get it down over the bulge of his erection, he wasn't sure what exactly she meant to *get off.*

So that he could prolong this past the foreplay stage, Declan reversed their positions again and helped her with the jeans and boots removal. Her hands were frantic now. Something he understood. Everything inside him was yelling for him to be inside her.

They were lying diagonally across the bed, and he groped behind him to open the nightstand drawer while Eden tackled his boxers. The need and urgency made them both a little sloppy, and her fingernails nicked his upper thigh. He didn't even feel the pain. The only thing he could feel was her beneath him.

Somehow he managed to grab a condom and get the darn thing on. And he could have sworn a lightning bolt hit him when he finally got inside her.

Yeah. Perfect.

This was special all right, and even though this fire made him stupid, he could still see that.

He forced himself to take a deep breath. Just so he could savor her and this for a few seconds before the breakneck pace started again. In those seconds, their gazes met. Declan saw the heat, of course. Saw Eden's amazing face. But he saw something else. Some emotion that he hadn't expected to see there.

This wasn't just sex for her.

Normally, that would have caused him to pull back, because he never wanted to lead a woman on. He'd never looked for anything permanent.

Still wasn't.

But there was something in the way Eden was looking at him that made him wish that he was doing that. That their situation wasn't what it was.

Then she lifted her hips, started moving and all thoughts of emotions and wishes went right out of his head. The need took over and dictated the speed. Dictated everything. Eden and he moved together with just one purpose.

To finish this.

It didn't take much. Probably because their foreplay had lasted two days, but Declan felt her climax ripple through her. It ripped through him, too, and brought him right to the edge.

However, before he went over, he leaned down and kissed her. Really kissed her.

It was Eden's taste in his mouth. The feel of her shattering around him. And the sight of the sight. He couldn't hold on any longer. So Declan took the plunge.

And landed right in Eden's waiting arms.

Chapter Sixteen

Eden's eyes flew open, and she bolted to a sitting position. Her heart was racing. Breath, too. She'd had a nightmare that had already faded, but it still caused the panic to rise inside her.

"It's okay," Declan murmured, and he pulled her back to him.

She glanced around. Then at him. It was dark, but she remembered she was in his bedroom. In his bed.

And they were both stark naked.

With the effects of the dream gone, her body relaxed. How, she didn't know. She'd never suspected she would be able to relax around a naked Declan. However, the thought had no sooner crossed her mind when Eden felt that trickle of heat.

A familiar one.

She let herself slide right back into that heat, and against Declan.

His eyes were closed, but he gathered her deeper into his arms and planted a lazy kiss on her forehead. "I'll get up in a minute."

Eden wanted to nix that idea right away. She wanted to stay like this, well, probably a lot longer than Declan did. He was a love-'em-and-leave-'em type. But she wasn't. It'd be hard when he walked away from her. And he would walk. Once this investigation was over, there'd be no reason for him to stay in her life.

Talk about a mixed bag.

The danger would be gone, but so would he. That put a pain in her chest as if someone had clamped a meaty fist around her heart.

Great.

Now she'd completely fallen for him.

The exact opposite of what she'd told herself to do.

Declan groaned softly, gave her another kiss. Not so soft and sweet this time. And he pulled away from her so he could sit up. He swung his feet off the bed, and she got a good view of his backside when he walked to the adjoining bathroom. He came back a few minutes later.

Still naked.

But this time she got a great view of the front of him.

He smiled, gave her another kiss and started to dress. Peep show was over, and Eden could only hope that they'd get to do this again.

"How soon will this be over?" Eden couldn't believe she'd blurted that out. And clearly she'd confused Declan because he just gave her an odd look.

He stood there, wearing just his boxers and that puzzled look. "I'm guessing we're not talking about the danger here?"

"No. Sadly, we aren't." She tried to wave him off, but Declan came closer, eased back on the edge of the bed. "Just so you know, I don't expect anything."

Mercy, she was babbling. And saying really stupid things.

"There's an old saying," she mumbled. "If you want to get out of a hole, the first thing you should stop doing is digging. I should stop digging."

The corner of his mouth lifted in one of his body-tingling half smiles. "You want to get out of that hole?" he asked.

And now she was the one puzzled. "I've done a thorough background check on you. I know you don't stay in relationships for long."

Now it made it sound as if long was what she wanted. And maybe she did. But that was a lot to dump on him after just having sex.

Incredible sex.

But it'd been just that once.

"Can we just forget everything I've said for the last five minutes?" she asked.

The smile returned, and he kissed her. All right. That made things better. The heat returned, too, washing away her blabbering.

"We'll talk soon," he promised. But then his forehead bunched up.

"You don't have a clue what you want to say to me," she guessed. It was apparently a good guess because he lifted his shoulder.

"I know I want to keep you safe." He glanced down at the scar on his chest. "And I know what happens when I lose focus. Not because I don't trust you," he quickly added. "I do. But I need to find this killer first. Then I'm thinking I'd like you back in my bed."

The next kiss he gave her left no doubts about that. Better yet, it cleared her own doubts. If sex was all that became of this, then it would still be some of the best memories of her life.

"You can stay in bed if you like," he offered, standing and continuing to dress. "You need the rest."

So did he, but he was obviously getting ready to work, and that meant she needed to work, as well. She got up and gathered her clothes, too, and was nearly dressed by the time Declan fished his phone from his pocket.

"No calls," he said under his breath.

So they hadn't missed anything. Again, a mixed bag. A good update on the case would have been a nice bonus.

Declan placed his phone on the nightstand while he strapped on his holster. Then he scrolled through the numbers on his phone and called Clayton. Because he put it on speaker, she could hear the ringing.

But Clayton didn't answer.

He tried Harlan next. But he got the same results. By the time he made it to Dallas's number, Declan was cursing.

"Something's wrong."

Eden moved closer and saw him try Stella next. Unlike the others, the woman answered on the first ring.

"Did you find him?" Stella immediately asked.

That question caused Eden to pull in her breath. Stella's tone was frantic, and it was obvious that something was wrong.

"Find who?" Declan asked.

"Kirby." Stella made a hoarse sob. "You don't know what happened, do you?" She didn't wait for him to answer. "I told Clayton you had your hands full guarding Eden. And besides, I thought you'd need some… distance."

"What the heck are you talking about, Stella!" No longer just a question but a demand. "What happened to Kirby?"

"Someone called him on his cell phone here at the hospital about an hour ago. I don't know who. Kirby said it was private and asked the guard to take me to the cafeteria for a while. When we came back, he was gone. His gun was missing, too."

"Gone?" Eden and Declan said in unison. Mercy, this couldn't be happening.

"How could he go anywhere?" Declan continued. "He's weak, going through chemo."

"Well, he somehow managed to get out. Or else someone took him. There was no sign of a struggle," she quickly added. "And he left me a note. He said he had to confront this killer once and for all."

Declan groaned. Then cursed. "Where'd he go?"

"I don't know, but Clayton and the others are looking for him."

"I'll call you back," Declan snapped. He hung up and fired off a text for Clayton to call him ASAP. He then sent the same text to the rest of his foster brothers.

The seconds crawled by, and Eden considered trying to reassure Declan that everything would be okay. But that would be a guess at best. A lie at worst. Because this sounded far from okay.

"I need to go look for him," Declan said. He glanced back at her. "And I don't want to leave you here."

She nodded. "I want to go with you."

Neither of them had to say that it might not be safe to do that. It didn't matter. Her father was out there, too, but he wasn't sick. He could fend for himself. It wasn't the same for Kirby, even though he'd apparently taken his gun with him.

The wait for a call from one of his brothers turned into what seemed an eternity, but Declan's phone finally buzzed, and she saw Wyatt's name on the screen.

"What happened?" Declan asked the moment he answered.

"We're still not sure. We don't think Kirby was kidnapped, but it's possible."

Declan's mouth tightened, his only visible reaction,

but she could feel the tension coming off him. "How did Kirby get past the deputy?"

"He got called away right before all of this happened. He said he thought the call was from dispatch, but it turns out it wasn't. It's possible Kirby was responsible for that, too."

It took Declan a moment to get his teeth unclenched. "But why the hell would Kirby do this?"

"We're not sure—yet. But we were able to put a tracer on his phone so we know where he's going." Wyatt paused. "Declan, Kirby's heading out to the abandoned Rocky Creek Children's Facility."

DECLAN COULDN'T GET Eden in the truck fast enough, and he gunned the engine so they could speed away. He had to get to Kirby, to stop whatever the hell was going on. But he had to be smart about this, too.

"This could be some kind of trap," he told her. "Keep watch around us." He'd do the same. But it might not be enough.

They were both armed, but it was getting dark, and their attacker could have set all of this up just to lure them out from the safety of the ranch. That nearly caused Declan to turn around and head back. He could leave Eden with the ranch hands.

But that could be a trap, too.

What if all of this was designed to get them apart? So that someone could pick them off one at a time? Besides, Eden wouldn't stay put while he went after Kirby. Declan was sure of that. She would try to help him, and in doing so, she could get herself killed.

Later, he'd curse himself for that. He shouldn't have slept with her. Should have kept this professional. But even now, with the unknown and the fear eating away at him, he knew that would have been impossible. From the moment he'd seen her on his back porch, he'd wanted her. And yeah, that didn't make sense, but then attraction rarely did.

"What would cause Kirby to go to Rocky Creek?" Eden asked.

Declan was still trying to work that out. "Maybe he didn't go voluntarily."

In fact, that was his first guess, because even if Kirby had learned the identity of the person who wanted them dead, he was too weak to go after him or her alone. He would have called one of his foster sons.

Unless he had believed his sons would refuse to let him go.

Which they all would have done.

They would have fought this fight for Kirby and forced him to stay at the hospital even if they'd had to cuff him to the blasted hospital bed.

"But why Rocky Creek?" Eden's gaze fired in all directions on the isolated country road. Keeping watch. "If he's doing this of his own free will, or even if someone took him, why go there?"

Declan had a theory about that. A bad one. "Maybe it's where Jack would have taken him to force Kirby to confess to Webb's murder."

Of course, that would only happen if Jack had been the one to kill Webb and now he wanted Kirby to take the blame.

But why do it this way?

A confession from his hospital bed would have accomplished the same darn thing. And why would Kirby have agreed to a confession anyway? Kirby was just as much of a suspect as Jack. Maybe more. And there was no physical evidence that Declan knew of to cause either of them to be arrested.

So what could Jack have on him that would make Kirby do this?

Eden made a sound to indicate she was thinking about his answer. "If Jack threatened to exchange your life for a confession, maybe Kirby's out here to meet him. And kill him."

Yeah. Declan's mind had already gone in that direction, and it wasn't a comforting direction to go. Kirby had been a good shot in his day, but this was no longer his day. Not with the cancer making him so weak. If he'd gone to Rocky Creek for a showdown, then it was a fight he could easily lose. With any of their suspects. Heck, even Beatrice would be able to outshoot him.

Declan's phone buzzed, and he put it on speaker as fast as he could. "It's me," Wyatt said. "Harlan, Dallas and I are at Rocky Creek. We had Clayton and Slade stay with Stella in case she's in danger. They're taking her back to the ranch."

Good idea, and Declan was glad his brothers were thinking more clearly than he was. That could be part of the trap, to divide and conquer, and if the killer managed to get Stella, it would give him or her a bargaining chip that could turn out to be a deadly one. All of them, including Kirby, would do whatever it took to protect Stella. Of course, Declan could say the same for Eden.

"We found Kirby's truck," Wyatt continued. "It's in a ditch about a quarter of a mile from Rocky Creek Facility. The engine's still running. The headlights are on."

Not good. That meant Kirby had exited in a hurry. Or had been forced from the vehicle.

"Any sign of footprints?" Or blood. But Declan didn't

have to ask that specifically. If it was there, Wyatt would let him know.

"No footprints. But there are drag marks."

Hell. That was not what Declan wanted to hear. Beside him, Eden pulled in her breath.

"The drag marks end just a few yards from the car," Wyatt added. "Looks like maybe someone picked him up and carried him, but the footprints have been brushed away."

"Kirby could be anywhere on the grounds," Declan grumbled.

"Yeah," Wyatt confirmed. "Dallas is headed to the main building. Harlan's taking the area near the creek. I'm going to the west side of the grounds."

"Eden and I will search the east side. We're just a couple of minutes out."

Declan shaved some time off those minutes by pushing even harder on the accelerator. He prayed there wasn't any ice on the roads, because he was taking the curves way too fast. He took the final turn on what had to be two wheels, but then had to slow on the uneven surface. It wouldn't do Kirby any good if they ended up in a ditch.

"Mercy, there are a lot of trees and shrubs," Eden said, looking out the window.

There were. Too many places for someone to hide. "When we get out, I need you to stay behind me, and if anything goes wrong, I want you to hit the ground. Agree, or it's the only way I'll let you out of this truck."

She nodded, but he didn't have time to push his point any further. Ahead, he saw Kirby's truck, and yeah, it was indeed in the ditch. The headlights cut through the dusk-gray winter landscape and created an eerie effect. Like stepping into a horror movie.

Wyatt was nowhere in sight, but Declan hadn't expected him to be. They were all out looking for Kirby, and he prayed that one of them would find the man alive and unharmed.

"Stay close," Declan reminded her. He grabbed the flashlight from the glove compartment in case the search went on longer than the twilight, and he shoved some extra magazines of ammo into his pockets. Eden did the same.

When he got out, the bitter wind nearly robbed him of his breath. Man, it was cold, and even though they were wearing coats, this still wouldn't be a pleasant search.

Declan made sure she was behind him, and they headed east. There were no buildings out there, but as Eden had noted, there were trees. Plus, there was a fence, and it, too, would make a good hiding place.

"Keep watch behind us," he whispered, and he got them moving fast. They had a lot of ground to cover. Acres. And with the wind howling, it would make it hard to hear if someone sneaked up on them.

He shoved aside a low-hanging branch, ducked underneath and saw the clearing just ahead. Declan stopped, tried to listen, because the clearing would be a good place for an attacker to gun them down. But there were no signs of anyone.

Declan turned on the flashlight and fanned it over the ground.

Footprints.

Definitely not drag marks, and they appeared to be fresh.

"Could they be Kirby's prints?" Eden whispered.

He shook his head. "Too big." And judging from the depth of the impressions, it was possible that this was someone who was carrying Kirby.

That sent his heart pounding against his ribs. Did that mean Kirby was hurt? Or worse? But Declan forced those questions aside. He couldn't help Kirby if he didn't focus solely on the search.

And on keeping Eden safe.

Because he darn sure didn't want her hurt because of some bad blood between Kirby, Jack or Leonard. Beatrice, either. Though if it was Jack's wife behind this, she'd obviously hired some muscle since she couldn't have carried Kirby from his truck.

"Move fast," Declan told her, and he turned off the flashlight.

He pulled in a hard breath and got them running toward a cluster of trees just on the other side of the clearing. Each step was a risk, and with each step he prayed that he didn't regret what he was doing.

Declan pulled Eden behind one of the larger oaks, and he took another second to try to hear anything that might be going on around him. Hard to hear, though, with his heartbeat crashing in his ears.

However, some movement caught his eye.

It must have caught Eden's, too, because she pivoted in the direction of another cluster of trees that was about twenty yards away. Even in the dim light, Declan could see the man.

Not an attacker.

Kirby.

Eden started to bolt toward the man, but Declan held her back so he could assess the situation. Hard to do with his foster father—correction, his father—so close.

Kirby was on his feet, leaning against a tree, and his arms were moving. His head was down with his chin practically touching his chest. No one was around him. At least no one that Declan could see.

Without taking his attention off Kirby and their surroundings, Declan eased his phone from his pocket and hit the first button. Wyatt's number. His brother answered almost immediately.

"We found Kirby," Declan whispered. "He's about a quarter of a mile from the road where I left my truck. Get here as fast as you can."

"Is he hurt?" Wyatt asked.

"I'm about to find that out now. Hurry," Declan repeated, and he ended the call so he could put his phone and the flashlight away. He wanted his hands free in case this turned into an attack.

Unfortunately, there was yet another clearing between Kirby and them. Not a wide one. But it was just enough to get them killed. Declan couldn't risk Eden's life like that, so he put her between him and a tree. That way he could take what he hoped would be a lesser risk.

"Kirby?" Declan softly called out.

He lifted his head. Not easily. "Declan." His voice sounded as weak as the man looked, and Declan wasn't sure how he was staying on his feet.

"Who did this?" Declan asked.

Kirby shook his head. "A lackey. All muscle and no talk. Don't know who he's working for because the guy didn't say a word."

Declan hoped they could soon remedy that. "Can you make your way to us?"

"Can't." It took him a moment and several labored breaths to continue. God knows what this cold and stress were doing to his body. "Someone tied me here."

Hell. This just kept getting worse.

"We have to go to him," Eden insisted. "We can get on the ground and crawl."

It wasn't a good plan, but it was better than darting

across the clearing. Besides, there wasn't much of an alternative. He couldn't leave Eden here alone because it might be part of the plan to grab her, too.

"Come on." Declan dropped to the ground and pulled her beside him. It wasn't easy. The ground was frozen and rocky, but they crawled toward Kirby.

Declan braced himself for an attack, but it didn't come. Thank God. They made it to Kirby, and Eden immediately started working to undo the rope that circled Kirby's chest and stomach.

"Are you hurt?" Declan asked, praying he wasn't.

"No. Just ready to fall flat on my face."

Yeah, he looked it. "What the hell happened? Why are you out here?"

"I got a call. Someone using a voice scrambler, but I think it was Jack. The person said I could end the danger to your life with a simple meeting. And a confession to Webb's murder."

Then the call must have been from Jack. But Declan rethought that. If it was Jack, why use a voice scrambler unless the man just wanted to throw them off his trail? However, there was someone else who could want that confession.

Beatrice.

Maybe so she could protect her husband from a murder rap. If she was so inclined.

Of course, Leonard could be the culprit, too. There were only two reasons for a suspect to use a voice scrambler. To muddy the waters or conceal their identity. But whoever was behind this, Declan intended to make them pay.

Eden finally got the rope undone, and Kirby practically dropped to the ground. Both Declan and she stopped that from happening by looping their arms around him. Even though Kirby had on a coat and his Stetson, he was freezing. That sent a new round of rage through Declan. This winter air could literally kill him.

"What now?" Eden asked.

Declan didn't want to go back through the two clearings with Kirby in tow, so he pulled them all as close to the tree as he could manage. "We'll wait for the others. They should be here soon."

He hoped.

That hope had barely had time to cross his mind when he heard the sounds. Footsteps, maybe. Maybe just the wind rattling the bare branches of the trees.

But the chill that went down his spine said it was something bad.

"Get down," Declan told them. And it wasn't a second too soon.

The shot blasted through the night air.

Chapter Seventeen

Eden tried to do what she could to protect Kirby, but despite his weakened condition, he'd have no part of that. He dragged her to him, shielding her with his body while Declan took aim in the direction of that shot.

Another bullet came their way, smacking into the tree. Then another. And it was that third shot that made Eden's heart go to her knees.

Because the angle had been different.

And that meant there wasn't just one shooter, but two. At least. All three of their suspects had enough money to hire plenty of assassins, so heaven knows how many had been paid to come here and kill them.

"Eden?" someone called out.

She hadn't thought it possible, but that got her heart racing even faster. It was her father.

What the devil was he doing here?

"Are you all right?" he shouted. He was somewhere to their left, in the direction of the fence. None of the shots had come from there, but he'd had men with him back in the woods near Maverick Springs.

Mercy, she hoped it wasn't them firing now.

"Don't answer," Declan warned her in a rough whisper. "I don't want anyone pinpointing our position."

It was a good argument, but she hated for her father

to think she'd been shot and therefore couldn't answer. Of course, that wasn't the worst of her fears. Her father couldn't be behind this attack. He just couldn't be. Whatever hatred he had for Declan, he wouldn't have gone this far with it.

She hoped.

But the little seed of doubt was there, and it tore away at her heart.

"Who's doing this?" her father asked.

But no one answered him. Well, no human anyway. Several thick blasts tore through the air. And this time they didn't come at Declan, Kirby and her—they went in her father's direction.

No. Someone was trying to kill him.

Kirby held on to her, maybe because he thought she might bolt from cover to help her dad. She couldn't. It'd be suicide, but she had to look for a way to end the danger now.

"My father's not behind this," she whispered. And she hated there was surprise mixed with the relief in her whisper.

"I got a call about an hour ago," her father continued. Judging from the sound of his voice, he'd moved. "The person said you were here at Rocky Creek and hurt and that you needed help."

And he'd come. Part of her was thankful for that, but another part of her wanted to throttle him for falling for such a thing. Declan and she had had no choice but to come after Kirby, but obviously someone had gotten her father here under false pretenses, since she hadn't been in need of help an hour ago.

She needed it now.

They'd need a miracle for all of them to get out of this alive.

But in a sick way it made sense that their attacker would want her father here. Both Leonard and Jack had a beef against him, and including her father and her in this dangerous mix would be a way to get total revenge.

The shots started up again. Mercy, did they. They came at them from both directions, and Declan, Kirby and she had no choice but to get flat on the ground. Maybe, just maybe, the gunmen wouldn't use that opportunity to close in on them.

"I can stop this," Kirby said. "It's me they want."

"You don't know that," Declan snapped. And when Kirby tried to get up, both Eden and Declan kept him on the ground. "You don't even know who's behind this."

"I know it's someone after me. Jack wants to kill me because of Stella. But not before he can get me to confess to Webb's murder. I can bargain with him to get you and Eden some time to escape."

"And if it's not Jack?" Declan didn't wait for him to answer. "Beatrice has several possible motives of her own. To get back at you for her husband's broken heart over Stella. Or to frame her husband for your murder. And then there's Leonard. Maybe he was lying about wanting to watch you suffer. He could have just waited until he had everything in place to come after you for killing his son, and if so, he's not the least bit interested in negotiation."

Kirby gave a weary sigh and quit struggling.

Good. At least Declan had put an end to that, but it didn't lessen the danger. For any of them. She prayed that her father would stay down and not try to do anything heroic to save her.

Even over the roar of the nonstop shots, she heard Declan's phone buzz. Because he had his focus on the gunmen, he handed her the phone.

"It's Wyatt," she relayed when she saw the name on the screen.

"Tell him and the others to stay back," Declan insisted. "I don't know how many shooters are involved or where they are."

Eden repeated that to Wyatt. "Best not to fire unless you have to," Wyatt answered. "I'm not exactly sure of Harlan's and Dallas's positions."

She ended the call, and even though Declan hadn't fired, she told him what Wyatt had said. It caused him to mumble some profanity, and she knew why. Not only were they pinned down in the freezing cold with a sick man, now they couldn't even return fire.

"I have to take out one of these guys," Declan said. "Use this if you have to. Just keep Eden safe." He reached in his boot and took out a small gun from the holster there. He handed it to Kirby.

But before Kirby could even take the weapon, Eden was shaking her head. "You can't go out there, Declan. You could be killed."

He leaned over, brushed a quick kiss on her mouth and levered himself up.

"You can't do this," she tried again.

But he got to a crouching position anyway. He did stay behind the cover of the tree, but he wouldn't have that meager protection for long.

"I'll sneak up behind one of them," Declan explained. And he got ready to move.

However, before he could go an inch, she heard a sound. Not the shouts and not a person's voice.

But a car engine.

The vehicle wasn't on the road, though. She could see the headlights slashing through the woods. And so was the vehicle. It was weaving in and out of the trees, the underbrush scraping against the sides like nails on a chalkboard.

"Maybe it's one of your brothers," Eden suggested.

If so, they were moving right into the line of fire.

The shots continued, and perhaps some of them were being fired into the approaching truck. It was hard to tell even after the vehicle came into view.

"Hell," Declan said. "That'd better not be who I think it is."

Kirby lifted his head and looked out. He cursed, too. "Stella."

Oh, God.

Had Stella really come or had she been brought here? Eden prayed not, but her prayers weren't answered. A moment later, the truck window inched down.

"I'm here to trade my life for theirs," Stella shouted.

The last word had barely had time to leave her mouth when the bullets began to tear through her truck.

"GET DOWN!" KIRBY yelled to Stella.

Once again, Declan had to stop the man from bolting into the clearing. But then Eden had to stop Declan. Every instinct inside him shouted for him to protect Stella. Maybe because she was a woman. Maybe because she was his mother. It didn't matter which—Declan had to force himself to stay put and try to figure out what to do.

He had to take out the shooter.

Why the devil was Stella here anyway? How could she have thought it would help to walk into this mess?

Of course, she might not have been thinking with her head but rather her heart. That particular organ was what had brought Declan out here. To save Kirby. Well, apparently Stella had the same notion. But there was one huge problem with that. She was now smack-dab in the middle of gunfire.

Eden still had his phone, and he glanced at it, then her. "Call Wyatt. Tell everyone to get down."

She did that immediately, but while he waited for his brothers to comply, the shots were continuing to slam into Stella's truck. Any one of those bullets could kill her.

If they hadn't already.

"Stay down," Declan warned Kirby and Eden.

He came up on one knee, took aim at the shooter to the right of the truck. And he fired. Declan couldn't actually see the guy, but he must have come close to hitting him because the shots stopped.

Well, on that side anyway.

They continued on the other, so Declan sent a bullet that way.

It worked. For a few seconds. Then the shots started again. His phone buzzed, too, and Eden answered it.

"Wyatt says he's dead center behind the truck," Eden relayed. "He's moving in closer to see if he can get a better shot."

Good. Declan kept his aim to the right and sent another two rounds that way. As before, the shots stopped, and when they started again, he realized the shooter had moved. Farther from the truck.

But closer to them.

Declan tried to keep himself positioned between Kirby and Eden, but then Eden lifted her head. "Dad, if you're still out there, get out of the way!" And she took aim at the left side of the truck and fired.

"What part of stay down didn't you understand?" Declan snarled.

But then Kirby fired, too, using the backup weapon

Declan had given him. He aimed at the same spot as Eden, and his shot smacked into one of the trees.

Hell's bells. He had a mutiny on his hands.

Declan was about to verbally blast them both, but he heard some profanity and didn't think it was coming from his brothers. Maybe one of the shooters had been hurt. Maybe either Eden or Kirby had managed to do one of them some harm.

"It's me!" Wyatt shouted, and he sounded close, probably right next to the rear of the truck.

And the next shot definitely came from Wyatt and went in the direction where Declan had been shooting. Eden and Kirby continued to fire, and soon the only shots were theirs. The footsteps confirmed they had the gunmen on the run.

"Cover me, Harlan!" Wyatt yelled.

Until then Declan hadn't realized Harlan was so close, but that was much-needed backup. Declan waited a few seconds. Then more. And when there were no shots fired, he got down on his belly so he could make it out to the truck.

Eden caught his arm to stop him, but Declan shook his head. "I have to make sure she's all right."

Her grip melted off him, and instead she held on to Kirby, probably because he had the same plan to check on Stella. Declan gave Eden one last look, thanking her, and he started to crawl across the clearing.

He didn't have to crawl far.

The truck door opened, and Stella stepped out. Or rather she staggered out. It was dark now, but thanks to a hunter's moon, Declan had no trouble seeing the blood on the right sleeve of her coat.

"I've been shot," she managed to say.

Declan jumped from the ground and raced to her.

He got to her just as she was collapsing, and she landed right in his arms. Cursing and praying, he scooped her up and ran back to cover.

"God, she's hurt," Kirby said, and he just kept repeating it.

Declan kept watch around them, knowing this would be the perfect time for an ambush, but he also kept glancing at Stella. She was pale. Her breathing was thin, and there was too much blood.

While Kirby cradled the woman in his arms, Eden called an ambulance. Of course, she had to tell the medics about the shots being fired, and that meant they wouldn't come close until the danger had passed. That couldn't happen soon enough or Stella might bleed out.

"Hold on," Declan told Stella, and he leaned out from the tree, trying to listen for any signs of those gunmen. He had to stop them, and that meant killing them.

"Go," Eden said to him, obviously figuring out what he had to do. "I'll protect them."

And she would. He had no doubt about that, but that didn't mean the gunmen couldn't get off some lucky shots. Still, it was an offer he'd have to take.

"Thanks." Declan brushed a quick kiss on her mouth and hoped he got the chance to give her a real thank-you later. She was putting herself in further danger to protect his family.

Declan stepped out of cover. Lifted his head. And he heard something. Not footsteps or voices. But some kind of crackling noise.

And then he smelled the smoke.

It seemed to come right at them in a thick wave.

"Fire!" Wyatt shouted. "Get the hell out of there now, Declan."

Declan saw the flames. Orangey red and thick in the

treed area to the right of them. It wasn't an ordinary fire. No. Not this. The flames shot up toward the sky.

Someone had set off a firebomb.

"This way." He helped Stella and Kirby to their feet and was about to head straight ahead to the truck.

But there was another of those bursting, crackling sounds, and the fire shot through that part of the woods. And worse, toward the truck. If the flames got to the gas tank, it'd explode.

No doubt what their attackers wanted.

"Change of plans," Declan said.

With Eden on one side of Stella and Kirby on the other, they started to the left. Toward the fence and the general area where they'd last heard Eden's father. If he was still out there, maybe he would decide it wasn't a good time to settle an old score with Declan.

However, they'd only made it a few steps when he heard a familiar sound that he damn sure didn't want to hear.

Another blaze roared up on their left.

And worse.

There was a fourth fire. The flames burst up behind them, and the smoke came at them from all sides.

They were trapped.

Chapter Eighteen

Eden looked all around them, and the terror rushed through her. The fire was everywhere. So was the smoke. And there was no visible escape route.

Sweet heaven.

Her father was out there somewhere, and he was no doubt in the middle of this, too. All of them could be killed, and they might never learn the reason for their deaths.

"Come on," Declan said. He hauled Stella into his arms and tried to help Kirby.

"I'll do it," Eden insisted. Declan had his hands full, and if they stood any chance of surviving, they had to move fast.

But in what direction?

There didn't seem to be a way out.

Worse, the smoke was rolling all around them. Smothering them. Eden choked back a cough, but Stella and Kirby weren't so lucky. Both of them started coughing.

Eden looped her arm around Kirby's waist. She couldn't carry him the way that Declan was carrying Stella, but she could help support his weight so he could move faster.

"This way," Declan ordered. "We have to get away from that truck before it explodes."

Oh, God. She hadn't considered that yet, but with her heart bashing in her chest and the adrenaline spiking through her, it was hard to think straight. Thank goodness Declan didn't seem to be having that trouble, even though she could see the terror on his face.

"Keep close," he added, "so we won't get separated."

The smoke would make it easy for that to happen. However, it wasn't so easy to keep up with him, either. Declan bolted toward the fence area. Where her father had been. There seemed to be just as much fire and smoke there as everywhere else, but maybe he'd seen some kind of opening.

Declan maneuvered them around a large tree. Then another. With each step the smoke thickened, making it harder to breathe. Kirby's coughing got worse, and he practically sagged against her.

"Leave me," Kirby insisted.

"Not a chance." If she couldn't save her own father, then she would save Declan's, though it broke her heart that she couldn't do both. Maybe, just maybe, her father had managed to get away before the firebombs had exploded.

Declan hurried, cutting through the seemingly endless line of trees. Did he know where he was going? Possibly. After all, he'd lived on these grounds when he was a kid, so maybe he knew a way out of all of this.

Stella moaned and dropped her head against Declan's shoulder. He mumbled something that Eden didn't catch, but she thought it might be a prayer.

"Declan?" someone shouted. It was Wyatt. He'd no sooner called out when there was another shot. Not a firebomb this time.

But a bullet.

And it'd been fired very near the sound of Wyatt's voice.

Now she prayed. Over half of Declan's family was in these woods, and heaven knew how many gunmen there were, ready to kill them if the fire didn't do that first.

Declan cursed but didn't answer his brother. No doubt because it would pinpoint their location and cause someone to fire at them, too. That was the last thing they needed.

Kirby stumbled, his legs giving way, but Eden caught him before he could hit the ground. She tried to get moving as fast as she could, but when she looked up, the thick smoke made it impossible to see Declan.

No!

She couldn't call out to him for fear of the gunmen. So she hurried. Or rather she tried to. But what remained of Kirby's strength was fading fast. Still, she didn't give up. Eden adjusted her arm around him, trying to keep her shooting hand free in case they were attacked, and she trudged forward.

With the smoke, she had no sense of direction, but she simply used the trees for cover and took it one frantic step at a time.

But that ended much too soon.

The flames shot up directly in front of them.

She pulled Kirby to the side, barely in time before the fire could burn him, and they ducked behind another tree.

"Gasoline," Kirby mumbled.

Yes, she smelled it, too, and she suspected it'd been poured on the ground. That would account for why the fire was moving in such a straight line. Of course, that line wouldn't last long because the fire would eventually burn through the dead leaves and limbs that littered the ground. It was freezing cold but dry, and that would only fuel the flames. The wind would, too.

They didn't have much time to get out of there.

She kept moving, though her lungs were burning, starved for air, and the muscles in her arms and legs were knotted.

"Eden?" she heard Declan say. Not in a shout but a rough whisper.

Despite their circumstances, the relief flooded through her, and she felt it even more when she spotted Declan just ahead. He caught her arm and pulled all of them behind an oak.

"You should save yourselves," Stella told them.

Kirby echoed that, but Declan obviously had no plans to listen. Good. Eden couldn't live with herself if she survived this ordeal at their expense.

Declan got them moving again, and they skirted along the lines of fire. Their attacker had obviously used a lot of gasoline, because she could smell it over the thickening smoke.

The sound blasted through the air, and even though Eden had tried to brace herself for pretty much anything, she hadn't braced herself nearly enough for that jolt that went through the entire woods.

"Stella's truck," Declan said.

It had obviously exploded, and she hoped no one was near it. Well, except for the gunmen. Maybe it had taken one or more of them out, but she doubted they would get that lucky. No, whoever was behind this attack had almost certainly planned an escape route.

Declan had to dodge another fire line, and they came out into a clearing. Except it wasn't very clear because of the smoke. He moved faster now but kept checking over his shoulder to make sure Kirby and she were keeping up.

They were.

Barely.

Her muscles were more than knotted now. They were cramping to the point of excruciation, and just when she thought she couldn't take another step, Eden saw some hope.

The white wooden fence.

She remembered it from their drive to the facility and thought it rimmed the entire property. But more important, it was next to the road. Maybe they could follow it back to Declan's truck and escape.

A howl of sirens cut through the other noises. The ambulance was already there. Nearby anyway. It couldn't approach until it was safe.

Whenever that would be.

Declan hurried to the fence and laid Stella on the ground. Eden did the same, and they both looked around to get their bearings. Not much to get, though. The smoke wasn't as thick here, and there was no sign of the fire. Good. It was a break they needed.

But then, Eden heard the sound.

Not the crackling flames. Not Stella's labored breathing. This was footsteps, and not just one set of them. Two or more.

Eden lifted her gun and tried to take aim. But it was already too late. The three men wearing dark clothes stepped out from the smoke. Like demons. Except those were real guns they were carrying. And they aimed those guns right at them.

"You can drop your weapons *now*," one of them said. "Or die right this second. Your choice."

DECLAN FROZE, BUT only because he couldn't get his weapon turned on all of the gunmen at once. He could take out one of them. Maybe even two. But that would leave a third one to start shooting.

That was a huge risk to take.

Of course, surrendering his weapon could be an even bigger risk, since he doubted these guys were just going to let them live.

So why hadn't the gunmen just opened fire?

Declan didn't know, but he figured that meant their boss had other plans that didn't involve a quick death. Maybe a slow, painful one so he or she could get the revenge they wanted.

He glanced around, looking for any way to escape. There were some more trees just to their left and near the fence. There was a ditch, too. Both might provide some cover if bullets started flying.

"My mother's hurt," Declan said to whoever could hear him. It was the first time he'd ever called her that, and the timing sure sucked, but maybe they'd be more receptive to what he was about to suggest if they thought of her as a mother and not their hostage.

Declan tipped his head to the end of the road. He couldn't see the ambulance, but judging from the sound of the sirens, it was there. "Let the medics come in and take both my father and her."

Again, it was the first time he'd called Kirby that, and he saw the tears in both Kirby's and Stella's eyes. Later, Declan would tell them that he no longer held a grudge for the secret they'd kept. Nearly dying put a lot of things in perspective.

Including Eden.

Here she was, her gun still aimed while she kept her

arm around Kirby. Protecting him. Just as she'd done on this entire nightmarish trek through the fiery woods.

And it could cost Eden her life.

Declan wasn't sure he'd get the chance to make that up to her, but he'd try. Yeah, he had things he needed to say to her, and somehow he had to create the chance for all of them to get out of this alive.

"Let the medics come and get my parents and Eden," he bargained. "Then we can talk and try to work this out."

Of course, letting the gunmen walk away from this was out of the question, since the trio could already be charged with multiple felonies. Also, none of them were wearing masks. Not a good sign. Because that meant they wouldn't want to leave any witnesses behind. Federal marshals and a P.I. would be huge loose ends.

"No way," the gunman in the middle said. "Just put down the guns."

"And then what?" Eden asked. "You shoot us all in cold blood?"

Declan didn't want her egging them on. Hell, he wished he could dig a hole and shove her in it. But he doubted Eden was going to let him do this by himself.

Nope.

She stood, slowly, and positioned herself arm to arm with him.

"Put down the guns now!" the man yelled. He took aim at Stella. "Or she gets another bullet. This one might not kill her, but she'll wish she was dead."

Declan had no doubt that the guy would shoot. Hell, maybe he'd been the one to shoot Stella in the first place. That didn't help quell the anger that rose hot and bitter in his throat.

"Go ahead," Kirby said. God, his voice was weak,

and this stress wasn't going to help matters. "Declan and Eden, do as they say. Put down your guns."

He glanced down at Kirby and saw the barrel of the backup weapon he'd given him. Kirby had it hidden under the edge of his coat.

Declan wanted to curse.

Normally, he would have liked having Kirby cover his back, but he doubted the man's hand was steady enough. Besides, if Kirby fired, those goons wouldn't waste a second shooting him.

"Do as they want and surrender your gun," Declan said to Eden. "But try to keep it close," he added in a whisper.

She gave a shaky nod, and she stooped to lay the gun on the ground just a few inches from her feet. Declan figured the guys would tell her to give it a good kick, but all three just looked at him.

"Your turn," one of them said to him.

Declan repeated Eden's movement, keeping his gun within stooping distance. Of course, that was way too far away if these guys started shooting.

"Anybody else got a gun?" someone called out, and it wasn't one of the goons.

It was Leonard Kane.

He stepped from the trees and drifts of smoke, and despite his earlier collapse at the hospital, he no longer looked weak and sickly.

Just the opposite.

He looked like a man pleased with himself.

And Leonard wasn't alone. He had another big, hulking gunman by his side. His, no doubt.

"You bastard," Stella said, and despite her injury, she tried to get to her feet, but thankfully Kirby kept her on the ground. At least that way they could scramble into the ditch if necessary.

And Declan figured it would become necessary.

He only prayed that Kirby, Stella and Eden could move fast enough when the bullets started flying again.

"Your lover there is the bastard," Leonard argued. "He killed my son."

"And hurting Declan won't bring him back," Eden snapped.

"No, but it'll make me feel a hell of a lot better." He sounded amused that Eden would give him an argument at a time like this. "Killing you will, too, because I know it'll get back at Zander for being such a jackass and trying to ruin my business. It's not enough for him to face attempted-murder charges for that witness."

"You set that up," Declan challenged.

"Yeah, I did. So what? Zander's still not behind bars, and that means he didn't get the payback he deserves."

Eden just shook her head. "You're dying. What good would revenge do now?"

"Well, for the short time I got left, it'll do a hell of a lot of good. Don't want to go to my grave without settling these last scores."

"And that score's with me," Kirby offered. He didn't get up, probably because he was still hiding the gun, but he did face Leonard head-on. "Let everybody go, and you and me will *settle* this. Here's your chance to finish me off."

"Too easy," Leonard answered. "Like I said, I want you to suffer. Besides, if I'd wanted you dead, I would have killed you a long time ago when I had Declan's parents killed. Oops. I guess that would be his adoptive parents, since he's your brat."

Stella cursed him again, and inside, Declan felt much

more than profanity. He'd spent a good deal of his life thinking about how he'd deal with the man who'd killed his adoptive parents.

And now he had the chance.

Except he couldn't take it without risking another set of parents and Eden. It cut him to the core that he couldn't just lash out at this SOB. But somehow, he would get that chance. Leonard was going to pay for all the misery he'd caused.

"I covered my tracks," Stella said. She was crying now. "There was no way you could trace his adoptive family to Kirby and me."

"Well, you sure didn't make it easy. I'd heard rumors that you'd had a kid, and I just kept digging. Didn't find anything for years, and then Beatrice stumbled onto the passport you thought had been destroyed. She did all the legwork for me."

"Beatrice was in on the murders?" Declan asked. Because if so, she'd pay, too.

"No. She's all talk, always whining about the money that she doesn't want to share. She found you, but all she'd planned to do was make sure Jack never located you. He was looking, too. So Beatrice set out to make sure no one ever found the passport or any link that would come back to Jack."

Declan wished that Beatrice had succeeded. But if she had, he would have never met Kirby. Never learned the truth about his parents.

And he would have never met Eden.

Of course, if he hadn't, Eden might not be on the verge of being killed by a revenge-seeking lunatic.

"And what about Jack?" Eden asked. "Did he help you with this plan?"

"Please." Leonard stretched that out a few syllables.

"I wouldn't trust that fool to take out my trash, much less put together something like this. A plan like this takes coordination. And hatred. A whole lot of hatred," he added through now-clenched teeth.

So according to Leonard, no one else was involved. That didn't make this situation less dangerous, not with those guns aimed at them. But Declan had to find a bargaining tool.

"If you kill me and leave Kirby alive to suffer," Declan said, "he and my brothers will track you down."

"They'll try," Leonard calmly. "But after this, I plan to leave the country and die in a quiet peaceful place, far from the long arm of the law." He paused. Lifted the gun he'd been holding by his side. "And now it's time for you to die."

"No!" Stella sobbed.

"Get them out of here first," Declan bargained. "Eden, too. No need for them to see you put a bullet in me." And that didn't mean he was surrendering.

No way.

If he had the others safely out of the way, then he could try to fight back.

"Everyone stays and watches," Leonard insisted. "And just so I can give you a little extra jab, Declan, I'll have Eden done first."

No. That couldn't happen. He couldn't lose her.

Leonard nodded. That was it, the order for her death. And the gunman in the middle, the one who'd issued those earlier threats, turned the gun on her so fast that Declan didn't have time to react.

The shot blasted through the air.

And Declan heard himself yell while he tried to push Eden out of the path of that bullet.

Chapter Nineteen

Eden braced herself for the pain. And for death.

The blast came. Loud and thick. Seconds before Declan knocked her to the ground. Even over the sound of the shot, she heard him shout her name.

But the bullet didn't go into her. The only pain she felt was from the impact of the fall.

Around her, everyone was scrambling. Declan, Kirby. Even Stella. They were all going for the guns, and it took her a moment to realize what was happening.

The man who'd tried to shoot her dropped face-first, his gun clattering away from him. Someone had shot him.

But who?

She didn't see anyone, but Eden didn't look that hard. She went after her gun instead. After all, Leonard was armed, and so were his three remaining goons.

The goons scrambled to the side behind some trees, and Leonard did, too, while he cursed a blue streak. Declan snatched up his gun, and in the same motion, he shoved Eden down into the ditch. Before she could get her own gun.

"Get Stella and Kirby," Declan told her, and she grabbed for them. Thankfully, they'd already started in her direction. Now she had to get Declan there, too, but he waited until they were all stashed behind the meager cover before he scrambled in with them.

One of the gunmen fired, but he missed Declan. That didn't stop him from trying again, though. But his weren't the only shots. There were others coming from the back part of the woods, where the smoke was still thick.

"Kirby, call off your boys," Leonard snarled. "Or they all die tonight."

"I'm not one of Kirby's boys," someone shouted back. Her father.

He was alive. But he was also close, right in the thick of this, and calling out to them meant Leonard's hired guns could pinpoint his position and kill him.

"I took out one of your men," her father added, "so why don't you come after me instead of my daughter?"

"No," Eden said. She didn't want this. She didn't want any of them to be in danger, but she was glad that her father had managed to take out one of them. Now hopefully it wouldn't make him a quick target for the gunmen.

"Maybe one of your brothers can take out the rest of Leonard's hired help," Kirby mumbled.

Eden wished the same thing. But it wouldn't be easy since they had to get through that fire.

"Put your hand on her shoulder to try to slow down the bleeding," Declan said to her. He tipped his head to Stella.

The bleeding was worse and Stella was shivering. Maybe going into shock. They needed to get her into an ambulance right away. Eden scooted closer to the woman and pressed her hand over the wound.

"Finish them," Leonard said to his men. "I'm gettin'

the heck out of here." And Leonard headed out with his bodyguard right by his worthless side.

Declan moved as if he might go after the man, but he glanced back at them. And instead of bolting, he took aim at the gunmen behind the trees.

The shots started.

Those gunmen began shooting at them, forcing Declan lower into the ditch so he couldn't return fire.

She heard Declan's phone buzz, and since he was busy watching to make sure those gunmen didn't come any closer, she took it from his pocket.

"Wyatt," she answered after she saw his name on the screen.

"Where are you?" Wyatt asked.

"Pinned down by the fence. Stella's hurt."

"How bad?"

Because Stella and Kirby were hanging on to every word, Eden would lie. "She'll be fine, but she needs a doctor." She ducked when a bullet tore up the chunk of the grassy ditch just above her head. "My father's here. Somewhere. And he took out one of the men, but Leonard's getting away. He's the one behind this."

Wyatt mumbled some profanity. "We're on the way. If possible, have Declan hold his fire so he doesn't hit one of us."

But before she could relay that to Declan, he fired. And for a good reason. One of the gunmen had run closer to them, ducking behind another tree. He was trying to move in for the kill.

"Just get here," she said to Wyatt, but he was no longer on the line.

More shots came. Closer than before. The gunman had obviously gotten into a better position. Eden's chest was tight from her pounding heart, and her breath was too fast. She tried to make herself settle down, but it was impossible.

It didn't help when Kirby levered himself up and returned fire with Declan's backup weapon. Both Declan and she pulled him back into the ditch, and that minimal effort seemed to exhaust him.

"Get down, Eden!" her father shouted.

That was the only warning they got before she saw him come out from the trees, and he started firing at the gunmen.

He took out the one nearest to them.

The other turned, took aim at her father. But Declan took care of him.

He double tapped the trigger, and the third gunman went down.

Eden said a prayer of thanks, but before she could even finish it, Declan was out of the ditch.

"You're not going after Leonard." And she tried not to make it sound like a question.

But that was exactly what he was doing.

"Wait with them," he said to her father. "And call the ambulance and tell the medics it's okay for them to come closer."

Good. The ambulance was nearby, waiting for the gunfire to end, so it shouldn't take long to arrive. But having her father stay with them meant Declan planned to do this alone. He wasn't going to wait for his brothers, probably because he knew every second counted. If Leonard managed to get away, they'd probably never catch him.

And a killer would go free.

God knows how long that would eat away at Declan. Probably for the rest of his life, and it wouldn't matter that the brain tumor would soon take care of Leonard.

Eden called the medic, relayed Declan's message and then got to her feet.

"I have to go," she told her father. She took the gun from Kirby's hand. "Stay with Stella and Kirby until the ambulance gets here."

Of course, if Declan's brothers got there first, they'd have to arrest Zander, but that wasn't something she could worry about right now. Declan was about to face down his own personal demon.

Her father tried to grab her arm to stop her, but Eden got away from him and hurried after Declan, who already had a good head start on her. Leonard had backup, and Declan would need it, too. Of course, he wouldn't want it. Not from her anyway. Still, she caught up with him just on the other side of the clearing.

"Go back," he ordered.

"Only if you will," she argued.

He kept walking, but he also looked all around them. Until then, she hadn't considered that Leonard might try to ambush them. She figured he'd get out of there fast.

But the sound had her rethinking that.

More footsteps just ahead.

Declan yanked her behind a tree and peered out.

"Looking for me?" someone said. Not ahead of them. But behind her. And it wasn't Leonard or any of Declan's brothers. This must be the bodyguard Leonard had with him.

Eden was between Declan and the man, so she snapped toward him, and she gave him a split second glance to make sure it wasn't someone they knew. It wasn't.

She fired.

So did he.

But Eden dropped down and fired again. The man

dropped, too, but before he even hit the ground, there was another shot. Not the gunman's. This one came from in front of them and smacked into the tree. It missed Declan's head by what had to be a fraction of an inch.

Declan cursed, shoved her all the way down and returned fire.

There was little smoke here. The wind had carried it in the other direction. So she had no trouble seeing Leonard in the moonlight.

"I won!" Leonard shouted. And he fired a second shot at Declan. "You and Kirby will have nightmares about me for the rest of your life."

Leonard took aim at Declan again. Declan aimed, too. He was the first to fire.

And Declan didn't miss.

She saw the look of startled surprise on Leonard Kane's face, as if he hadn't expected to die. Not ever. And a single word of profanity left his mouth as he slumped forward.

Declan didn't even wait a second. He hurried first to the bodyguard and touched his fingers to his throat.

"Dead," Declan mumbled. And he raced to the clearing to do the same to Leonard. Eden kept her gun aimed just in case the bullet hadn't killed him.

But it had.

As she'd done with Leonard, she looked at Declan's face but saw no relief there. No sign of victory.

"Stella," Declan said, catching onto her arm. They started to run. "We have to get Kirby and her to the hospital now."

Chapter Twenty

Declan sucked at waiting, but he wasn't the only one. Like him, Eden was pacing in the hospital waiting room.

Dallas was on his umpteenth call with his wife. Clayton, too. Both had plenty of nervous energy coming off them. Slade wasn't pacing or chatting on the phone, but he had his wife, Maya, wrapped in his arms as if a hug could bring them some peace.

Maybe it could.

Because the pacing and the nonstop phone conversations sure weren't working.

Only Harlan and Wyatt were seated. Wyatt had his legs stretched out in front of him, his Stetson over his eyes, but Declan figured he wasn't getting much rest. Neither was Harlan, and it was likely to stay that way until they got some news about Stella and Kirby. They both had to be all right, and even though Declan didn't want his mind to go in that direction, he couldn't help but think the worst. Stella had lost a lot of blood, and Kirby was weak from the cancer. God knows what this ordeal had done to him.

"How the heck did Stella get away from you?" Declan asked Clayton once he was off the phone. He extended that question to Slade. After all, both of them had been at the hospital guarding her.

"She's sneakier than she looks," Clayton grumbled.

"And faster," Slade supplied, not sounding at all pleased that he'd been outsmarted by a woman twenty years older than he was. "Once we got her back to the ranch, she slipped out through the kitchen and jumped in her truck. She drove away before we could stop her."

"We had no idea she'd try something that stupid," Clayton added.

Yeah, it was stupid all right, but Declan looked at his brothers' faces. Both Slade and Clayton were parents now, their sons tucked safely at the ranch with their nannies. And Declan was betting that his brothers would do anything to save their children.

Even something stupid.

"At least now we know why Declan's so hardheaded," Harlan added.

Declan appreciated the insult. Coming from a brother, it was practically mandatory in situations like these. However, it didn't help cut through the worry that any of them were feeling.

"Both Kirby and Stella will be okay," Eden tried to assure Declan. She maneuvered her pacing closer to him and brushed her hand over his arm. It helped. But not enough.

There was worry all over her face, too, and like Leonard had said, this would give them enough nightmares for a lifetime. Thankfully, Eden's sisters were okay. Declan and she had confirmed that with a phone call on the drive to the hospital.

"I should have been able to protect everyone better," he told her. "Including you."

She lifted her shoulder. Gave a weak smile. "We're in one piece. I'd say you did a pretty good job."

Now, that gave him some comfort. She didn't hate

him for the mess he hadn't been able to prevent. Because he thought they both could use it, he leaned in and kissed her. If that garnered anyone's attention, they didn't say anything.

Harlan, however, grunted. "Maybe no one will shoot at us today."

Wyatt put his thumb to the brim of his Stetson and eased it back a bit. "I get shot at all the time."

"A lot of things happen to you that don't happen to normal people," Harlan grumbled. "It's that pretty face of yours. Too pretty to be a lawman. Just makes people want to shoot you."

Declan was thankful for the brotherly ribbing. It was an attempt at normal when the situation was anything but.

"The cold weather slowed the bleeding," Eden added in a whisper. She put her arms around him. "Plus, Stella's otherwise strong and healthy."

Both true. But it crushed his heart to think of her in surgery to remove a bullet put there because a man believed he needed to avenge an old wrong.

Declan heard the footsteps in the hall, and everyone turned in that direction. Hoping for news. But it wasn't the news they were expecting.

It was Sheriff Geary and Zander Gray.

Eden went to her father, hugged him and some of the worry faded from her expression. "I didn't know if I'd get to see you before they took you to jail."

Declan hadn't been sure of it, either, but if the sheriff hadn't brought Zander by the hospital, then Declan would have taken Eden to the jail as soon as they had word about Stella and Kirby. It didn't matter what differences Zander and he had had. Eden loved him, and she deserved to see him before he was whisked away.

"The murder charges will be dropped," Declan explained to Zander. "Leonard confessed to hiring someone to kill the witness, and he did that to set you up so that you'd look guilty."

Zander nodded. "Thanks."

"Don't thank me yet. You'll still have to serve time for the original charges." But maybe it wouldn't be much. He no longer had a burning desire to see justice served when it came to Zander.

Because he was Eden's father.

And it would hurt her to see him behind bars.

Still, she seemed to accept that jail time was inevitable, and she left her father's side to return to Declan's. She slipped her arm around his waist again.

"I'll talk to the D.A.," Declan continued, talking to her father, "and tell him you helped us stop Leonard and his hired guns." He paused. "Thank you for protecting my parents during the gunfight."

"Thank you for protecting my daughter."

Declan hadn't expected Zander's thanks to mean that much. But it did. "It wasn't a chore."

"Yeah, I can see that." His gaze turned to Eden. "Come and see me when you can."

She nodded, but anything she was about to say was cut off by more footsteps. This time, it was Dr. Cheryl Landry, and she no doubt had an update about Stella and Kirby. Declan couldn't tell if the news was good or bad from the look on her face.

"Stella's asking to see you," the doctor said. "All of you." And she included Eden in the glance.

The sheriff took hold of Zander's arm. "We need to head out."

Eden mouthed a goodbye and *I love you* to her father, and then hurried down the hall with the rest of them. Declan braced himself for what he might see in the post-op room. He hated that this might be Stella's deathbed farewell.

But it wasn't.

She wasn't exactly sitting up and looking fit, but she was awake and smiling as much as she could, considering she'd recently come out of the operating room.

"The surgery went well," the doctor explained. "I was able to remove the bullet, and I don't think there'll be any permanent damage. She'll be here a day or two." She hitched her thumb to the corner of the room. "Him, too."

Only then did Declan see Kirby in a wheelchair.

"He insisted on being here." Dr. Landry frowned. "But now that he's sure Stella's going to be okay, I need to get him back in his own room. He'll need to stay overnight. He's fine. No injuries. It's just a precaution."

"I wasn't going anywhere until I knew she was okay," Kirby grumbled.

Stella's weak smile returned, and even though her eyelids were already drifting down, she motioned for Declan to come closer. When he did, she took his hand and gave it a gentle squeeze. "You called me your mother tonight. That's the first time."

He kissed her forehead. "Won't be the last."

And that was true. Nearly losing her had brought it all crashing down. In a good way, this time. He'd always loved Stella. Always thought of her as his protector and caregiver. Now he wanted some time to get to know her as his mother. The woman who'd made a lot of sacrifices to keep him alive.

And she had.

"Does this mean Declan will get special treatment now?" Wyatt asked, kissing Stella's cheek, too.

"All you boys are mine. He's just the only one who got my blood."

Clayton, Harlan and Dallas came forward to give her the same cheek kiss, and even though Stella was clearly enjoying the attention, at the moment she couldn't keep her eyes open.

"I need all of you out," the doctor insisted. "A recovery room means there's some recovering to do, and Stella needs that right now. But you can come back in the morning."

They would. Declan needed to have a long chat with Stella, but it could wait. For now, he leaned down and whispered in her ear, "I love you."

Despite her half-shut eyes, he saw the tears, but he thought they were of the happy variety. He made a mental note to tell her that more often.

When the doctor gave them another get-out order, his brothers began to trickle out, each of them stopping by Kirby first. No hugs. Kirby wasn't the hugging type, but Declan figured the man knew how they felt about him.

"You speaking to me?" Kirby asked when Declan stopped in front of him. "Because I could see why you wouldn't want to."

"I'm speaking to you all right, and I'm warning you to never again pull that sneaking-out stunt. You fought enough of my battles when I was a kid. You don't need to go fighting more."

Kirby nodded. Maybe thanking him. But probably not agreeing. If it came down to it, Kirby would fight for any of his sons, and Declan knew if their situations were reversed, he'd do the same thing.

"Well, I do have one battle left," Kirby said. "Webb's murder. The rangers aren't just going to drop this.

They'll keep looking for his killer, and they'll keep looking at all of us."

"We'll handle it when and if the time comes." Declan gave Kirby's shoulder a gentle squeeze. Not a hug, but close enough.

"I'm proud of you, boy. Proud of all of you."

Declan felt his own eyes burn. It wasn't that Kirby had withheld praise. He'd been plenty generous with it over the years. But it never got old hearing it from his father.

Eden gave both Stella and Kirby a kiss on the cheeks, and they left before Dr. Landry pushed them out of the room. Declan didn't feel the actual relief until he got into the hall where his brothers were waiting. And it hit him then.

They'd survived.

All of them.

"You okay?" Eden asked, and she took his arm, maneuvered him so that his back was against the wall. Probably because he didn't look too steady on his feet.

He managed a nod. He was more than okay. "I'm thinking we should start dating," Declan told her.

Dallas grumbled something he didn't catch. "I'm out of here. See you back at the ranch." Slade left behind him. Then Clayton.

But Wyatt stayed, as if amused by this.

Eden put her mouth directly to his ear. "Dating? But we've already had sex. Great sex," she amended in a whisper.

"Yeah, but we can still date, and then maybe you'll consider moving in with me. Of course, since I live in the sticks, you might not want—"

She stopped him with a kiss. A good one, too. "I'd love to move in with you."

All right. This was going pretty well. "Then maybe you'll fall in love with me. Hope so anyway. Because I'm sure as hell in love with you."

"You cursed when you said I love you," Wyatt pointed out. "Women don't like that."

Declan shot him a glare. "Don't you have someplace else to be, maybe some other shooting to get mixed up with?"

"Nope. Besides, I like watching my kid brother trip over his tongue." But he chuckled and looked at Eden. "Make him suffer a little. Wait a month or two before you let him know you're in love with him, too." He met Declan's gaze. "Because she *is* in love with you, you know. Or maybe you're just too dense to see what the rest of us already know."

With that, Wyatt strolled away.

"Are you in love with me?" Declan asked her.

"Yes." And she didn't hesitate, either. She even added another of those mind-numbing kisses.

Oh, man. This day had started like a nightmare, but the ending was getting better and better.

He'd never be thankful to Leonard for what he'd done, but it had brought them to this point. Of course, they would have gotten here anyway. He'd been crazy about Eden since he'd seen her on his porch.

Declan moved closer to her, put his mouth to her ear. "After you move in, I figure I'll give it a month or two, and then I'll ask you to marry me."

She smiled. "Then I figure I'll say yes. You're not getting away, Declan. I want you for life."

Life sounded pretty darn good.

Declan contributed one of those mind-numbing kisses, as well. Then another. Because she tasted so good and felt so right in his arms.

In fact, everything about this felt right, and that was the first time in his life he'd been able to say that. Declan pulled Eden to him and didn't let go.

* * * * *

Don't miss the heart-stopping conclusion of
THE MARSHALS OF MAVERICK COUNTY
when WANTED goes on sale next month from
USA TODAY *bestselling author Delores Fossen.*
Look for it wherever
Harlequin Intrigue books are sold!

REQUEST YOUR FREE BOOKS!
2 FREE NOVELS PLUS 2 FREE GIFTS!

✦ HARLEQUIN®

INTRIGUE®

BREATHTAKING ROMANTIC SUSPENSE

YES! Please send me 2 FREE Harlequin Intrigue® novels and my 2 FREE gifts (gifts are worth about $10). After receiving them, if I don't wish to receive any more books, I can return the shipping statement marked "cancel." If I don't cancel, I will receive 6 brand-new novels every month and be billed just $4.74 per book in the U.S. or $5.24 per book in Canada. That's a savings of at least 14% off the cover price! It's quite a bargain! Shipping and handling is just 50¢ per book in the U.S. and 75¢ per book in Canada.* I understand that accepting the 2 free books and gifts places me under no obligation to buy anything. I can always return a shipment and cancel at any time. Even if I never buy another book, the two free books and gifts are mine to keep forever.

182/382 HDN F42N

Name _____ (PLEASE PRINT)

Address _____ Apt. #

City _____ State/Prov. _____ Zip/Postal Code

Signature (if under 18, a parent or guardian must sign)

Mail to the Harlequin® Reader Service:
IN U.S.A.: P.O. Box 1867, Buffalo, NY 14240-1867
IN CANADA: P.O. Box 609, Fort Erie, Ontario L2A 5X3
**Are you a subscriber to Harlequin Intrigue books
and want to receive the larger-print edition?
Call 1-800-873-8635 or visit www.ReaderService.com.**

* Terms and prices subject to change without notice. Prices do not include applicable taxes. Sales tax applicable in N.Y. Canadian residents will be charged applicable taxes. Offer not valid in Quebec. This offer is limited to one order per household. Not valid for current subscribers to Harlequin Intrigue books. All orders subject to credit approval. Credit or debit balances in a customer's account(s) may be offset by any other outstanding balance owed by or to the customer. Please allow 4 to 6 weeks for delivery. Offer available while quantities last.

Your Privacy—The Harlequin® Reader Service is committed to protecting your privacy. Our Privacy Policy is available online at www.ReaderService.com or upon request from the Harlequin Reader Service.

We make a portion of our mailing list available to reputable third parties that offer products we believe may interest you. If you prefer that we not exchange your name with third parties, or if you wish to clarify or modify your communication preferences, please visit us at www.ReaderService.com/consumerschoice or write to us at Harlequin Reader Service Preference Service, P.O. Box 9062, Buffalo, NY 14269. Include your complete name and address.

HI13R

***

When he was satisfied they were alone and there was nothing immediate for him to find, he hurried back to the living room and met Lyla's glare.

"Jonah Webb. He was the man from the orphanage who was murdered years ago."

She studied his face. Then his badge. "You're one of the marshals who were raised at the orphanage."

"Rocky Creek Children's Facility," he supplied.

He tried not to go back to those bitter memories. Failed. Always failed. But bad memories weren't going to stop him from doing his job. Wyatt went back to the center of the living room so he could keep watch to see what the bozo with the gun was going to do.

"Webb's body was found, what, about six months ago?" she asked.

"Eight. The Rangers are still investigating it."

"Your foster father is a suspect," Lyla whispered. "I remember reading that in one of the reports."

Yeah. Kirby Granger was indeed that. And worse, he might have actually done it, though Wyatt never intended to admit that aloud.

"I'm not sure what's going on," he said. "But I suspect you know a lot more than you're saying."

The remark had no sooner left his mouth when Lyla leaped to her feet and started toward the hall. Probably to get the .38 that was somewhere in her bedroom.

"Why are you doing this?"

"Why are *you* doing this?" And Wyatt dropped his gaze to her stomach.

"I don't understand." The words rushed out with her breath.

Maybe she did. Maybe she didn't. But Wyatt decided to test a theory or two. "I think you got pregnant so you could manipulate this investigation."

She stared at him as if he'd lost his mind. "My baby has nothing to do with Jonah Webb's murder."

"You sure about that?" he countered.

"Positive," Lyla mumbled, but there it was. The doubt that slid through those intense brown eyes. "Why would it? Why would my baby have anything to do with this?"

Wyatt took a deep breath. Had to. "Because that baby is mine."

***

Does Lyla know more than she's saying?
And what will happen to their baby?
Find out in USA TODAY *bestselling author*
Delores Fossen's WANTED, *part of her popular miniseries*
THE MARSHALS OF MAVERICK COUNTY,
on sale in January 2014!

RECOVERING A SPECIAL GIFT

Marcie Powers saw her son everywhere. For two years, no stroller or baby seat passed without his face. She saw him so much, not even her estranged husband, Joseph, believed her. So he wasn't surprised when she claimed to have found their son once again. Yet this time, she wasn't hysterical. There was something…different. And although she couldn't have known it, news of Joe's own secret parentage was about to hit Louisiana headlines—and it would put his son at risk for a big payday. Now Joseph and Marcie will have to trek through the bayou at the whims of a kidnapper to find the son they'd thought lost to them forever—and reclaim the love between them.

GONE
BY MALLORY KANE

Available January 2014, only from Harlequin® Intrigue®.